Killing the Carnations

A Heavenly Highland Inn Cozy

Mystery

Cindy Bell

CW00858441

ISBN-13: 978-1494791360

ISBN-10: 1494791366

More Cozy Mysteries by Cindy Bell

Heavenly Highland Inn Cozy Mystery Series

Murdering the Roses

Dead in the Daisies

Bekki the Beautician Cozy Mystery Series

Hairspray and Homicide

A Dyed Blonde and a Dead Body

Mascara and Murder

Pageant and Poison

Conditioner and a Corpse

Makeup, Mistletoe and Murder

Table of Contents

Chapter One

The Heavenly Highland Inn was bustling with activity. The lobby was flooded with businessmen and women in suits, waiting to have their turn at the registration desk. All hands were on deck to deal with the inundation that the corporate conference had created. Ever since a starlet and a well-known professional tennis player had tied the knot under the roof of the inn, the calls and requests for rooms had not stopped. With so much to juggle on her own, Sarah had finally given in and admitted she needed a little extra help. So, after organizing the conference itself, Vicky was right behind the front desk with her sister and Aunt Ida.

Aunt Ida was more interested in the handsome, young men that were lined up waiting to check in. She nudged Vicky lightly in her ribs with her elbow. "They didn't make 'em like this when I was young," she insisted. It was the same line that Vicky had heard several times now, but she still gave Aunt Ida a loving smile.

"Oh Aunt Ida, you're still young," Vicky said firmly as she tapped the keys on one of the computers behind the desk. Somehow two of the mid-level executives of the corporation had been double booked and she was trying to put out the fire before Sarah smelled the smoke.

Ballant Industries was one of the most lucrative up and coming corporations on the east coast, and it was a huge honor for the inn to be chosen to host their annual conference. It would span three days and include several meals, as well as entertainment that Vicky had arranged. It was a late booking as their previous venue had fallen through, but Vicky suspected they had switched at the last minute after hearing about the celebrity wedding.

"I don't understand what the problem is," the man before her said in a grating tone. He seemed to speak through his nose rather than his lips, and expected his polished demeanor to somehow be able to hurry things along.

"I just need one more moment, sir," Vicky replied calmly. Being on the front line at the reception desk was not Vicky's speciality. She could throw together an amazing party in less than twenty-four hours, but having patience with an impatient executive was very different from juggling caterers and decorators.

"Here we go," she said with a smile of relief as she managed to find an empty room on the second floor. "You'll be staying in room 203," Vicky offered a dazzling smile and handed the man the key for his room. Unlike many other hotels and inns, the Heavenly Highland Inn still used old-fashioned keys instead of electronic key-cards. The cost of updating the old inn to the technology they would need for the key-cards was far more than the cost of maintaining keys. No one seemed to mind the traditional technique of opening the door to their rooms, and it allowed them to keep the authentic feel of the inn itself, which had its own rich history.

The inn changed hands mostly through family lines, and most recently from the ownership of Vicky and Sarah's parents who had passed away in a car accident, to their young daughters who were not expecting the sudden responsibility. Though they had grown up in the inn, and both had spent the better part of their adolescence working behind the reception desk, neither anticipated what it would be like when the full ownership of the inn rested on their shoulders. Although Vicky wished for her parents' guidance quite often, she at least had the zestful, if not outlandish influence of her Aunt Ida, who had lived at the inn for as long as Vicky could remember.

"Excuse me," a voice said impatiently from beside Vicky. She glanced up to see the irate glare of one of the most powerful men on the east coast. Jeremy Minkle was the CEO of Ballant Industries, and certainly not someone that Vicky wanted to see upset. With his thick, dark waves of hair and his glowering, brown eyes, she would have considered him handsome, if he didn't look so irritated. She took a deep breath and reminded herself to try not to take his aggravation personally, everyone's nerves were on edge in the busy environment.

"Is there a problem, sir?" Vicky asked and tried not to sound impatient.

"Yes, there's a problem," Jeremy said sternly, his brusque tone indicating that he was used to being in charge. "I asked for the same room I stayed in last time I was here. That was a room with a view of the gardens and mountains. The room you sent me to has a view of the parking lot," he pressed his lips together tightly with annoyance.

Vicky searched for his name through the roster of past guests and found that Jeremy had indeed stayed at the inn the year before. She was surprised, because she didn't recall him staying and Sarah hadn't mentioned it. Unfortunately, the room he requested was showing as already occupied.

"Sir, I'm sorry but..." Vicky began to say, but she was interrupted by one of the maids who worked at the Inn.

"Oh, I'm sorry for the confusion," Emily said quickly, her gentle voice perfectly matched to the softness of her features. Emily was in her early twenties and had blonde curls that were always tied back in a bun, yet a few strands insisted on tickling at her cheeks and the corners of her eyes. She had the kind of voluptuous body that seemed to draw the attention of many of their guests, but instead of being arrogant about it, she was always very generous and docile. She was very artistic and she loved to paint every opportunity she got and was very talented at it.

"What do you mean, Emily?" Vicky asked as she studied the woman before her.

"I overheard Sarah saying that Mr. Minkle was going to be staying here again, so I took the liberty of booking him the same room, so that it wouldn't be given to someone else," she explained quickly and ducked her head to hide a slight blush. "I had trouble entering his details and Sarah was already so busy I didn't have a chance to get her to fix it, and Mr. Minkle left such a generous tip the last time he was here," she added in a lower voice. Vicky smiled a little at that comment. Emily was one of the more senior maids on staff so she had been trained in the booking systems to help out if they were ever desperate, but unlike painting, technology was not her strong point. Vicky assumed she was just trying to make sure she had the big tipper in her wing of the inn. It probably didn't hurt that Jeremy was so easy on the eyes either.

"That's just fine Emily, in fact it's perfect," Vicky nodded her head slightly as she retrieved the key for the room. "Would you mind showing Mr. Minkle to his room?" she suggested.

"I certainly can," Emily agreed. As she escorted Mr. Minkle away, Vicky was pleased to see that he appeared much more relaxed. She released a sigh of relief as they disappeared together into one of the elevators. The next couple that walked up to the desk caused Vicky to turn her head to keep from grinning. The woman was decked out in a gold dress, the skirt of which ended mid-thigh, paired with just as gold stiletto heels that added at least a few inches to her height. Her hair was bright red and pin straight, with straight cut bangs hanging right above her blonde eyebrows. Though she carried nothing, not even a purse, her husband was loaded down with several suitcases which he carefully placed on the floor in front of the desk.

"Our room please," he said with obvious exhaustion. He was a delicately framed man, with features to match. Though his physique caused him to seem a bit fragile his bold, blue eyes seemed to gleam with confidence and intelligence.

"Your name, sir?" Vicky asked with more warmth than she normally offered. She had sympathy for the man who was obviously worn out from waiting in line with so many bags.

"Charleston Davis," he said quickly and glanced over at the woman beside him. He smiled at her with a dreamy curve to his lips, and Vicky noticed that she wore an engagement ring. She understood now, that he was still trying to make a good impression. She could understand why, as the statuesque woman could have easily been a fashion model with her slender frame and wide vacant gaze. She didn't even flinch when a man beside her lost his balance beneath the large bag he was carrying and jostled her arm slightly. But Charleston did.

"Watch it, Brendan," he said sharply as he glared at the other man. Brendan stumbled a little and put the bag down on the floor.

"I'm sorry," he said respectfully to the woman who had yet to even blink. "I think I might have over packed," he chuckled with a good-natured smile. He reached up to straighten his midnight blue tie and smooth down the lapel of his black suit jacket.

"Having an entire wardrobe of tacky suits won't make you the next CEO," Charleston said sharply.

"I thought you were going to be the next CEO?" the woman beside Charleston asked accusingly. Suddenly Vicky was very aware of what was unfolding around them. She glanced up with surprise at the conversation, then quickly looked back down at the computer screen. It was important in the hotel business to try to stay out of the affairs of the guests. She did her best to, but Aunt Ida didn't seem to share the same standards.

"Would you look at that dress!" she called out with a gasp of pure pleasure. "What is it made out of, butter?" she asked with a purr as she ran her fingers across the shimmery material. Vicky's eyes widened in horror at her aunt's words, but the woman wearing the dress only lifted her chin upward with pride.

"It's nice isn't it?" she assessed Aunt Ida with a critical stare. "Yours isn't so bad either," she offered in a disdainful tone. It seemed as if her words were meant to be a compliment but it was hard to tell from her disinterested smirk.

"Thank you," Aunt Ida said and straightened the hem of the peacock blue blouse she had paired with a black pencil skirt. Vicky thought the blouse was a little overdone, as it actually included faux peacock feathers, but she kept that opinion to herself. Charleston and Brendan were still glowering at each other.

"We'll just have to wait and see, won't we?" Brendan asked as he arched a brow slightly at Charleston. Charleston pursed his lips as he snatched the room key from Vicky's hand.

"There's nothing to wait for Brendan, I'm a shoe in and you know it. The only reason you are even being considered is to avoid accusations of favoritism," he tilted his head to the side and smiled confidently as he looked at Brendan. "Don't worry, I'll make sure you have plenty of work to keep you busy and your mind off not being selected as the next CEO."

Brendan's eyes narrowed at that. Vicky noticed their cinnamon shade was muted by his thick and long eyelashes. He was older and rounder than his counterpart, his stomach protruding slightly against the buttons of his suit jacket that strained against his midsection. His features were rounder too, with soft full lips, a receding hairline that drew back from a rounded forehead, and even, small round ears that carried the arms of silver-rimmed glasses. His hair was very dark and cut short at the base of his neck.

He looked very professional, and though his appearance was rather unremarkable, the way he held himself with such patience and warmth endeared him to Vicky instantly.

"How generous of you, Charleston," he said with a small smile.

"Perhaps you have someone to help me with these bags?" Charleston asked.

"Of course," Vicky nodded. Aunt Ida was still fussing over Charleston's fiancée's dress and shoes.

"Do you think they'd make it in my size?" Aunt Ida wondered out loud. With Aunt Ida's slender frame, Vicky thought they would, but she couldn't imagine her aunt wearing it. Aunt Ida was a very alluring woman, she did her best to flirt with every available man she encountered, but Vicky assumed she might be a bit past the age that was appropriate for such a dress.

"I'll find out for you," the woman replied with a sweet smile. She seemed to be enamored with Aunt Ida which Vicky understood. Aunt Ida had a very charming and vivacious personality which made her rather endearing. Vicky gestured to the concierge who was standing nearby.

"Can you help Mr. Davis upstairs with his bags," she asked, trying to hide her amusement as Kent took one look at the pile and then grabbed a luggage cart.

As Charleston and his fiancée followed him, Brendan stepped up to the desk.

"Sorry about all of that," he said with a grim smile. "Charleston can get a little carried away."

"No need to apologize," Vicky smiled politely. "Could I have your name?"

"It's Nicholas Brendan," he replied and seemed to be studying Aunt Ida who was still standing beside the desk. Aunt Ida appeared to be oblivious to his attention as she was daydreaming about herself in that gold dress. Vicky noticed it however, and did her best not to grin.

"Well, Mr. Brendan I have two options for you. You can have a room on the third floor, or on the second," she tried to meet his gaze, but he was still staring at Aunt Ida. "Would you prefer a larger room with a view of the parking lot, or a smaller room with a view of the garden?" she asked calmly.

"The larger room is fine," he said with a shrug. "I can see there's more beauty to view around here than just the garden."

Aunt Ida glanced up at his comment and caught him looking directly at her. Her cheeks flushed with surprise but her lips curled into a come hither smile.

"Oh Mr. Brendan, I can show you to your room, if you'd like?" she suggested, her smile spreading and her lashes batting swiftly. Vicky suppressed a giggle and handed over Nicholas' room key.

"That sounds wonderful," he agreed and accepted the key. He offered Aunt Ida his arm, and she led him towards the elevator. As Vicky glanced back at the crowd of people in the lobby she noticed it was beginning to thin out. They were finally getting everyone checked in. She stole a glance over at Sarah and saw that she looked exhausted. Vicky made a mental note to make sure she got a day at the spa. Sarah's day didn't end when she went home, she still had a lot to take care of with a family and house to keep up. Her husband was helpful, but it was still a lot on her big sister's shoulders, and Vicky tried to do her best to make sure she got a little time away to herself.

Vicky on the other hand hadn't been getting much alone time, and she loved every minute of it. She and one of the deputy sheriffs had struck up a friendship that quickly developed into a romance. Vicky was so used to being on her own that being in a new relationship had been a bit bumpy for her at first, but she was getting very used to Deputy Sheriff Mitchell Slate always being there for her. She found herself eager to meet up with him in the evenings no matter how tired she was. That night would be no different as they had plans to go out for Chinese food together. The thought renewed her determination to get through the day.

As she registered several more people and distributed their room keys she noticed that several of the managers of the company had brought along their spouses. Maybe they had heard about the inn's reputation for being a romantic getaway, not just for the stars, but for anyone that enjoyed such a serene environment. The character of the old inn was enticing for many as its expansive stone structure could remind one of old French castles. But the charm of the inn itself wasn't the only thing that drew the attention of travellers. It was the setting that really pushed the inn to the top of the list when it came to an enjoyable escape.

Set on the outskirts of a quaint little town, the Heavenly Highland Inn was surrounded by nature at its finest. From the towering trees that were always laden with large and colorful leaves, to the mountains beyond the expansive gardens, there was something for everyone to enjoy. There were numerous walking trails that wound along a small lake and up through a few acres of woods, as well as leading directly through the well manicured gardens. The gardens were the inn's pride and joy as they always had colourful flowers no matter what the season. They were dotted with intricate stone statues that stood out as pleasant surprises amidst the foliage, as well as little nooks and hideaways where guests would often retreat for private picnics or trysts. The chef of the inn, Henry, offered a special picnic basket for any guest who wanted to enjoy the beauty that surrounded the inn. It was very popular with guests who were couples, but often even a single person would order the basket and spend the afternoon in the garden.

Sarah worked very hard to ensure that every guest who stayed at the inn had a memorable experience. Vicky worked very hard to ensure that whatever their special occasion might be, they had a wonderful way to celebrate it. They made a good team, as they were not just sisters, but also good friends. While Sarah tended to bring out the mature side of Vicky, Aunt Ida always sought to involve her in her antics and crazy schemes. Vicky was grateful to them both, and even her dear brother-in-law, Phil, who was as straight-laced as they come.

"Phew, that was quite a rush," Sarah said as she walked over to the desk. "Did everything go okay over here?"

"Sure," Vicky nodded a little. "Emily helped out with some room arrangements, but I think we're going to have our hands full with the CEO's two candidates for replacements."

"Oh?" Sarah asked with surprise and glanced around the lobby for any sign of them.

"Nicholas and Charleston," Vicky explained. "They're already headed up to their rooms," she lowered her voice slightly as her lips curved into a devilish smile. "Aunt Ida escorted Nicholas."

Sarah's eyes widened as she stared at Vicky. "Oh no! We're never going to get her away from him!" she laughed in a good natured way, but Vicky could see the exhaustion in her sister's eyes.

"Go home and rest, Sarah," Vicky suggested gently. "I'll take care of things here, and if there's a problem, I can always call you."

Sarah looked as if she might argue with Vicky, but she had to stifle a yawn first. "Thanks, Vicky," she murmured gratefully then gave her sister a warm hug.

Vicky turned back to the computer as Sarah walked out of the hotel. It paid to live where she worked. As long as there were no issues, Vicky could kick back in her own apartment which took up one section of the main floor.

"Hey there," Mitchell's voice drifted across the desk as he paused before it. When Vicky looked up she was immediately swept away by the warm smile that danced across his lips.

"Hey yourself," she replied with a soft laugh. "I didn't think you were going to be here until eight."

"I know I'm early," he grinned apologetically. "It's not my fault, I just couldn't stay away," he pouted playfully.

It took some major restraint on Vicky's part to keep from launching over the desk and jumping right into his arms. She cleared her throat and looked back at the computer monitor.

"That's all right, you can keep me company while I get things settled for the night," she suggested with a slight shrug.

"That would be perfect," Mitchell agreed as he glanced around the lobby. "So the big conference is off to a good start?"

"So far so good," Vicky sighed nervously. "Hopefully, all these high powered executives aren't going to turn out to be very picky and demanding."

"Hmm," Mitchell leaned his elbows on the desk and nodded as he studied her amorously. "I'm sure if they are, you'll set them straight."

"What's that supposed to mean?" Vicky asked with a grin.

"That you're a very resourceful, intelligent woman who can handle any situation that's thrown at her," Mitchell replied with complete confidence as he stared into her green eyes.

"Good one," Vicky laughed and leaned forward across the desk to softly kiss his cheek. It had been a long time since Vicky was in a steady relationship and things with Mitchell had certainly become steady. He always seemed to be looking out for her.

"I need about an hour," she murmured beside his ear before she turned back to the computer. "We'll have to have dinner at my place, because I sent Sarah home early. She was really wiped out."

"That was nice of you," Mitchell offered with a smile.

"How was the first day without Sheriff Mcdonnell?" Vicky questioned. Mitchell had been put in charge while the sheriff was having a couple of days off for a minor operation.

"Uneventful," he offered casually as he turned to look over the lobby of the inn. He had a habit of surveying everything wherever he was. It was something that Vicky hadn't noticed at first, but now she thought was rather adorable.

Chapter Two

Aunt Ida was on a mission of her own. She had led Nicholas Brendan to his room. As he unlocked the door he paused and glanced over at her.

"Thank you for your help, and the company," he said in a warm tone.

"It was no problem at all," Aunt Ida replied and tried to sound casual. The truth was she had enjoyed every minute of the elevator ride alone with him. He continued to compliment her on everything he could think of, and she found the incessant flirting to be very appealing. "If you need anything, feel free to ring the desk," Aunt Ida added and started to turn away from the door.

"Wait," he smiled coyly at her as she paused by the door. "Why not stay for a drink?" he suggested with warmth growing in his tone. Ida studied him for a long moment. She was always up for a little romance, but she had learned to be just a little cautious. She didn't know him at all, and though she found him to be quite attractive, she wondered why he would be so quick to invite her inside.

"Perhaps another time," she suggested as she started to step away from his door.

"Must it be another time?" he asked pleadingly, and his eyes crinkled at the corners in a way that made Ida smile. "Just one glass?" he nearly begged.

"Just one," she finally agreed with a giddy smile. As she walked into his room he held the door open for her. When she heard the door click closed she turned to face him, and found that he was smiling with admiration at her. She shivered a little as his gaze swept along her figure and then back up to meet her eyes.

"You know I was dreading this conference," he muttered as he walked past her towards the small refrigerator that he had requested be stocked with a couple of bottles of local wine.

"You were?" Ida asked with surprise. "Why is that?"

He pulled out a bottle of wine and opened it up with the corkscrew that had been left on top.

"Well, it's really just a charade, a send off," he explained as he popped the cork and took a sniff of the wine. "Mm, lovely," he shook his head with what seemed to be genuine surprise. "Who knew that my visit would be filled with such beauty, and such flavor," he added as he poured them both a glass of wine. When he turned with her glass, Ida was flustered. She was the one that usually did all the flirting, and to have him be so bold was both exciting and a little nerve wracking.

"Thank you," she murmured in response to the glass of wine and the compliment.

He sat down at the small table, and Ida sat across from him with her glass of wine. "Those carnations are so beautiful, just like you," he said moving a vase of carnations on the table to the side so he could look at her.

"They are from the surrounding gardens. I picked them this morning," she said with a smile.

"You still haven't told me why you weren't looking forward to your stay here in our inn."

"It's like this," he explained casually. "Jeremy is stepping down as CEO. He knows that he has to choose between two candidates to replace him. He can't just appoint someone, it has to look like he's thought it out, run it past the board, and really made a tough decision," Brendan chuckled at that and shook his head. "But we all know who he wants to take his place. He hasn't been shy about revealing how fond he is of Charleston. The fact that I was even chosen to be in the running was a bit of an honor, but I never had any illusions that I was going to be named CEO."

Ida narrowed her eyes as she tried to read the man's expression before her. She could sense some shyness, some low confidence in the way his lips shivered slightly and the wrinkles that lined his features in just the right places crinkled as he spoke. "Why do you think so little of yourself?" she questioned. "A handsome and intelligent man like yourself with many years of experience should certainly be in the running. Maybe you're not giving yourself enough credit."

"Oh, if you want to talk about intelligence Charleston is your man," Brendan said with a touch of confidence. "That man is a whiz, I tell you, and he's prone to bragging, but he has a right to. I appreciate your kindness, but I'm certain that you couldn't assess my worth to my company over one glass of wine," he smiled sheepishly.

"Maybe not," Ida agreed as she took a sip of her wine, before her voice grew smoky. "But I can certainly assess the handsome part." She laughed quietly as he blushed dark red like a tomato. "You're not accustomed to compliments are you?"

"Not from a woman as engaging and beautiful as yourself," he replied with a raised eyebrow. Ida giggled, she couldn't help it. She knew it ruined the intensity of the moment, but his suave demeanor and his wandering eyes were enough to make her tingle from head to toe, and unfortunately when she tingled, she also giggled.

"Now who's being kind?" she smiled a little and brushed her fingers back through her latest hairstyle. After an unfortunate incident that had left it a very unflattering color she had cut it short and dyed a honey blonde shade for the moment. It did make her appear even younger than she usually did, but she found the short cut that drifted against the base of her earlobes to be just a bit too young. As her hand swung back down towards the table Nicholas caught it with his own. His touch was feather soft.

"It's not kindness," he said firmly. "It's the truth. I don't think I've ever met anyone quite like you."

"Well, now that is something I believe," Aunt Ida grinned, her eyes gleaming.

***

Downstairs the lobby was still fairly quiet as Vicky tried to hurry through the last of the paperwork. Mitchell was patiently waiting for her, but she was impatient to spend some time with him.

As she finished up with her work a few of the staff members came to her with questions.

"Can you look over the breakfast menu?" Henry, the chef for the restaurant attached to the inn, asked.

"Sure," she took it and glanced over as Emily walked towards her from the other side of the lobby.

"Oh Emily, did you get Mr. Minkle settled in okay?" Vicky asked as she looked up from the menu. Emily's face was a little pale, as if she too had been run ragged by the evening.

"Yes, he's fine," she replied swiftly. "I'm going to head back to my room, if that's okay with you?"

"As long as everything's been taken care of for the evening that's fine," Vicky agreed quickly. Emily lived in the staff quarters that were located just outside the inn beside the gardens. "Are you feeling okay?" she asked with some concern.

Mitchell looked over at Emily as well. Emily looked away shyly and shook her head.

"I'm sorry it's just been a busy day and I'm feeling a little light-headed. I'd just like to lay down for a bit."

"Of course, I'll make sure no one disturbs you," Vicky said with a warm smile. Mitchell continued to study Emily.

"Do you want me to walk you to your room?" Mitchell offered politely.

"No, no thank you," Emily said quickly as she turned away from him. "I'll be fine by the morning I'm sure," she added as she hurried off through the side door of the lobby that exited out into the gardens.

"She's acting a little odd," Mitchell said with a slight tilt of his head.

"Oh, stop," Vicky rolled her eyes with a short laugh. "She's just worn out. That dreamy CEO seems to have a thing for her, maybe she had a little too much fun getting him settled in," she winked playfully at Mitchell.

"Dreamy CEO?" Mitchell replied abruptly with a hint of heat in his fierce blue eyes that was diminished by his laid-back smile.

"Dreamy to her I meant," Vicky giggled and finished looking over the breakfast menu. She marked a change to be made in the drinks they were offering as she knew that some of the executives enjoyed the fancier coffee drinks.

"Mmhm," Mitchell replied in a drawn out hum. He again swept his gaze around the lobby.

"Would you mind taking this to Henry for me?" Vicky suggested, hoping to keep him occupied with something other than surveillance.

"Sure," Mitchell took the menu and walked towards the kitchen. Vicky watched him walk away, her mind wandering to what she had in the fridge that she could cook for dinner. With a couple of candles lit and some nice music playing they could still have a very romantic evening.

***

Ida had nearly finished her glass of wine when Nicholas jumped up to pour her another. As he did he brushed his hand across his pocket, and then grimaced.

"Ida, I'm so sorry but I think I've left my wallet in the car, I'm just going to run down and see if it's there, do you mind waiting here a few minutes?" he looked at her imploringly. "I'd hate to let this ruin our time together, but I don't want my wallet to get stolen either."

"Oh, you don't have to worry too much about that here," Ida assured him. "Not much gets stolen. But of course I'll wait for you, I wouldn't want to be without my purse," she pointed out.

"Wonderful," he sighed with relief and set her now filled glass of wine down in front of her. "I'll be right back, don't disappear on me, all right?" he smiled at her again. Ida blushed and smiled in return. She hadn't been so catered to in some time, and she could certainly get used to it.

After Nicholas left the room she glanced around. He had yet to unpack or settle in so

31

there wasn't much for her to see. But she couldn't help being a little nosy. She walked over to his suitcase and just looked at how stuffed it was. She liked a man with a good sense of style. The outer pocket of the suitcase was unzipped and slightly open. She knew it was wrong, but that didn't stop her from tugging the lip of the pocket back enough to peek inside. What she saw was Nicholas' wallet. She was about to run after him when she realized how it would look if she declared she had found his wallet inside his suitcase. She didn't think that would bode well for a second invitation for drinks, or maybe even dinner. Instead she peeked a little further into the pocket. There wasn't much else inside it, aside from a toiletry bag, and what looked like a coin purse. She was going to investigate just a little further, when she heard the knob turning on the door. She jumped back into her chair and picked up her glass of wine just as Nicholas walked back inside. He had a distressed expression and was wiping his hands across his pockets repetitively.

"Any luck?" Ida asked, knowing exactly where his wallet was.

"I'm afraid not," he frowned and shook his head. "I swear I'd lose my head if it wasn't screwed on. My wife was always good at keeping track of things for me."

"Your wife?" Ida asked curiously. She hadn't noticed a ring on his finger.

"Yes, unfortunately she passed several years ago," he explained with a hint of grief in his voice. "She was a wonderful woman," his eyes hung on Ida's features as if there was something about her that reminded him of his late wife.

"Well, I think women have a knack for remembering things," Ida explained with a warm smile. "If I had misplaced my wallet, I would check all my bags. You know I have several different purses, and sometimes I place my wallet in one and forget about it for a few days, then I have no idea where I put it in the first place. So the first thing I do if it comes up missing is to check all of my bags," she said again. She hoped she wasn't hinting strongly enough to indicate that she might actually know where his wallet was.

"I always keep my wallet in my pocket," he shook his head slightly and then met her eyes again. "But I guess I should check everywhere."

As he walked over to his bag, Ida released a quiet sigh of relief.

"Well, look it is here!" Nicholas announced with joy. "I was just going to start cancelling credit cards! Ida, you truly are my good luck charm," he announced as he turned around to face her. He held out his hand to her, and she accepted it as she stood up from her chair. He continued to stare deeply into her eyes as he pulled her gently closer. Ida's eyes grew wide as her heart fluttered with excitement.

***

As Vicky was filing the last of the paperwork from her desk she heard the door between the bar and the lobby open. She looked up, expecting to find a last minute guest to register, what she saw instead was Charleston's fiancée. She was teetering on her high heels and being held up by a large-framed man in a business suit. His cheeks were flushed with exertion and he seemed to be having a hard time keeping her upright on her heels.

"Ma'am, are you okay?" Vicky asked as she stepped out from behind the desk to check on her.

She waved her hand dismissively. "Oh, I had a few too many drinks and the bartender kicked me out," she sighed. "But luckily this fine gentleman was there to save me," she smiled seductively at the man who still had her propped up on his arm. "My hero."

Vicky was acutely aware that the man was not Charleston.

"Well, I can help you up to your room if you'd like," Vicky suggested as she met the woman's eyes.

"No, I'll be fine," she assured Vicky. "I know what Charleston will say, he'll say Amanda, why must you always drink too much wine," she giggled and then lowered her voice as she whispered to Vicky. "I always tell him it's because I'm marrying you, Charleston," she laughed wildly and headed unsteadily for the elevator.

"Thanks for your help," Vicky said with a grateful smile to the man who had helped her into the lobby.

"It's no problem, we're used to Amanda," he shrugged mildly. "Poor Charleston has no idea what he's getting into though. At least he'll be CEO so he won't have too much to complain about," the man headed off towards the stairs. As soon as the elevator doors closed behind Amanda, Vicky wondered if it was a mistake to let her go upstairs alone. Would she even be able to find her room? She knew that Amanda wasn't going to accept help from her, but she hoped that she would from someone she obviously liked. She dialled Aunt Ida's cell phone, which was a device she was still getting used to. She answered on the third ring.

"Hello?" she asked, and then before Vicky could answer she growled. "Is this thing on? I can't even tell! Is that you Vicky?"

"Yes it's on, it's me, Aunt Ida," Vicky tried not to laugh. "Can you do me a favor?"

"Of course I can," she replied.

"Where are you?" Vicky asked.

"Uh," there was a pause, and then Aunt Ida muttered something under her breath. "I'm just leaving Mr. Brendan's room," she explained. Vicky's eyes widened at that, she had been up there for quite some time.

"Oh really?" she asked with a gossipy tone, but then she remembered that there was business to attend to so she moved on. "I just need you to see if you can find Charleston's fiancée, Amanda, remember you met her earlier today?"

"Yes I remember, how could I forget such a beautiful dress?" she sighed at the memory.

"She just headed up to her room, room 309, in the elevator but she's more than a little intoxicated so I'm worried that she won't make it to her room," Vicky explained, her voice fluttering a little with the anxiety she felt.

"Don't worry, I'll look after her," Ida assured her. When Ida hung up the phone she turned back towards Nicholas. The call had interrupted them just as he was leaning towards her. Ida was fairly certain he had intended to kiss her.

"I'm sorry but duty calls," she said nervously and twisted her fingertips through some of the material of her blouse. She hadn't felt so awkward since she was just a teenager.

"I understand," he said calmly, his eyes still locked to hers. "I hope that I'll have the chance to spend a little more time with you before this weekend's over."

"I would like that," Ida replied with a slow smile, "very much."

As she walked towards the door she heard him following her. He reached past her to open the door for her, showing he was a true gentleman.

As she turned to say a final goodbye, she found him waiting there for her, his lips poised to embrace hers. Ida was startled and swept away by the abrupt but soft and sweet kiss. It made her shiver with surprise and elation.

"I-I have to go," Ida stumbled over her words. He had her very flustered.

"I hope to see you again soon," he murmured and smiled at her as she hurried off down the hallway.

She heard him close the door and let out a long sigh. She had to pause for a moment to regain her composure. She thought the flirting had been fun, but he had been so bold as to kiss her, and that she had not expected. She reminded herself that Vicky still needed her help with Amanda and forced herself to start walking down the hall. She was almost at the elevator. Her heart was still racing from her encounter and the kiss that she had just shared with Nicholas. With her mind swimming she didn't notice the dark crimson stain at first, not until she stepped down in the middle of it, and the carpet gave a squishing sound. Her heart stopped in that moment and she looked down at the spreading circle that was a very different shade to the tan carpet that covered the hallway.

"Is that?" she asked herself nervously. She hoped she was wrong, and that what she saw was wine, but it didn't look like it was. She glanced up at the door it was spreading out from under to find that it was not quite closed all the way. When she tried to nudge it open with the toe of her shoe, it only pushed about an inch inward, before it thumped against something. Ida swallowed back a scream and with a trembling hand reached into her purse for her cell phone. She dialled Vicky's number. Vicky picked up on the first ring.

"Vicky, we have a problem," she said quickly. "Get up to the third floor, I'm calling an ambulance now."

She didn't even give Vicky a chance to respond, instead she dialled for an ambulance right away. She knew that whoever was behind that door was in desperate need of medical attention.

Chapter Three

When Vicky reached the third floor, her breath was short from taking the stairs and from panic. She didn't want to believe that this could be happening. But, Aunt Ida had certainly sounded serious when she spoke to her on the phone. As Vicky stepped into the hallway, she found Ida still standing in the hall, shoving her shoulder against the door.

"We have to get in," she said with a gasp. "Whoever is in this room is seriously hurt, and if we don't get in..."

"Aunt Ida," Vicky said gently as she drew her aunt away from the door. As her aunt stepped aside, Vicky began pushing against the door, too. When she finally managed to get whatever was behind it to budge slightly she braced herself for a groan or a cry for help, but there was only silence.

"Hello?" she called into the room. "Are you okay?"

"What is this?" a shrill voice asked from behind them. Vicky and Ida both turned suddenly to discover the woman in the gold dress. She still looked just as pristine but her brows were furrowed with annoyance.

"Why are you blocking my way?" she demanded as she tried to step past the two women. When she saw the blood spreading across the carpet she shrieked and jumped backward. It was an agile feat, considering the height of her heels and the fact that she was still obviously tipsy.

"What have you done?" she demanded. "Have you hurt my Charleston?"

Vicky's heart began to pound very loudly. She looked up at the room number. It was Charleston's room. Not only did they possibly have a murder on their hands, but it was the murder of a man who was next in line to be the CEO of a multi-million dollar company. She slammed her shoulder against the door just as the elevator dinged, alerting them to the arrival of Mitchell. Before Vicky could catch herself she nearly fell into the room. She caught herself with the doorknob of the forced open door, and stopped herself from landing directly on top of Charleston Davis, who was gazing up at the ceiling with wide empty eyes. Those eyes that had impressed her when she first saw them, the eyes that looked so intelligent and confident, were now dull and glazed. It was quite obvious that he had been murdered.

"Oh no," she said under her breath as she felt a strong grasp tug at her elbow.

"Come out of there, Vicky," Mitchell insisted as he gently pulled her away from the crime scene. Vicky was a little dazed at first, and glad that it was Mitchell's eyes she was now looking in to.

"What happened?" he asked her as he continued to hold her steady.

"I have no idea," she admitted as other officers brushed past her. "Aunt Ida was the one that found him," her voice wavered as she glanced back into the room. It was hard to think that the man she had just met was truly gone.

"Are you okay?" he asked and tried to meet her eyes. She nodded without speaking. Ida was trying to reassure Amanda who was getting more frantic by the second.

"No! He can't be dead!" she exclaimed, her voice rising. "We weren't married yet! He hadn't changed the will! He wasn't even a CEO!" she moaned and leaned heavily against Ida. Ida looked over at Vicky with astonishment. Vicky returned the shocked expression. She had heard of some cool and calculated women that married for the sake of money, but she had never seen such a careless display. Vicky walked over to her aunt and attempted to shift Amanda from her aunt's shoulder to her own.

"Amanda, let me take you somewhere quieter, is there anyone I can call for you?" she asked as gently as she could. Amanda threw her arms up into the air, brushing Vicky off her as she did. She glowered at Vicky and Mitchell who had straightened his posture and was prepared to restrain Amanda if he needed to.

"I don't have anyone," she hissed, and stumbled on her shoes. "He was all I had. Charleston. Someone took him from me!" she wailed. One of the EMTs walked up to her and spoke to her soothingly.

"Miss, why don't you let me take a look at you, okay?" he asked as he guided her towards the elevator. "We'll get you some water, and I have something you can take for your nerves."

Amanda reluctantly allowed him to lead her away, but she shot a withering glare over her shoulder at Vicky.

"I'm going to sue this place," she hissed.

Vicky tried to keep a poker face, as she knew she needed to remain professional, but she was so disgusted by the way the woman was not even concerned about her fiancé's death beyond the financial consequences, and then to have her threaten to sue her, Vicky's eyes naturally narrowed into a glare.

"Vicky," Mitchell said calmly from beside her. "Don't let her get to you, she's obviously drunk, and emotional. She won't be able to sue you."

"She might not be able to," a voice said from behind both of them. "But I'm sure my lawyers will want to know about this."

When Vicky turned to look she saw that it was Jeremy Minkle. "We booked our conference here assuming there would be sufficient security. You are housing some very wealthy and powerful people here, so how is it that someone can simply murder one of them?" he demanded as he stepped closer to Vicky. "We haven't even been here for a day!"

"Mr. Minkle, I understand you're upset," Vicky attempted to calmly explain.

"No, you don't," he growled in return and those brooding eyes that had been so attractive to Vicky earlier filled with fury. "You have no idea how upset I am. But you will," he added. "Trust me, you will."

"Oh Nicholas don't look!" Ida exclaimed suddenly as she saw him running down the hall.

"What's all the commotion?" he asked as he looked between Jeremy, Ida, and the officers that were moving carefully back and forth in the room.

"I'm so sorry," Ida said quickly. "It's Charleston."

"Charleston?" Nicholas asked with a gasp as he looked back at the body.

"Congratulations, Brendan," Jeremy said as he clapped the man hard on the shoulder. "Looks like you're going to be the new CEO."

Mitchell shifted his gaze sharply in Nicholas' direction as Nicholas looked up with a bewildered expression.

"I'm going to need to speak with both of you," Mitchell said in an even tone as he looked between the two men. "As well as anyone else that is here for the conference."

"You think one of us did this?" Nicholas said with shock in his voice. "Who could do something so..." he stammered as he searched for a word. Jeremy narrowed his eyes as he studied Nicholas.

"People will do the strangest things, for money," he stated grimly, clearing his throat. "But I doubt it was anyone from our company. However, whatever you need we'll cooperate. There's nothing to hide," he glanced over his shoulder at Vicky again. "My lawyer will be in touch."

Nicholas walked over to Ida and gently wrapped an arm around her shoulders. "Are you okay? A woman such as yourself should never witness something so terrible."

Vicky eyed the man suspiciously as he held her aunt close to him in his arms. But Ida didn't seem to mind one bit. In fact she rested her head on Nicholas' shoulder. It suddenly struck Vicky that she and Sarah always had someone to turn to. Sarah had her husband, and now Vicky had Mitchell, but Ida hadn't had a companion to rely on in quite some time. Vicky wanted to be happy for her aunt, but something about Nicholas left her uneasy. When Mitchell finished talking to the officers he walked back over to Vicky, his gaze still filled with concern.

"Are you really okay?" he whispered as he paused beside her.

"I will be," Vicky said but her voice was trembling. She stood nervously beside Mitchell as he rubbed her arm soothingly and tried to get her to look him in the eyes.

"It's going to be okay," he promised her. "We'll find out who did this."

"I know you will," Vicky said quietly and lowered her head. She wanted to let Mitchell soothe her, but it was very difficult to stop thinking about what she had seen. Not only was Charleston dead, but they had no idea who had killed him. As well-connected and high-powered as Jeremy Minkle was, could his threat come true? Would he sue them?

"Do you think we should evacuate the inn?" she asked him with a frown. "This huge conference is going on, it will be difficult to get everyone out smoothly."

"I don't think we need to do that," Mitchell assured her. "Not just yet, it seems to me that whoever did this had a target, and it was Charleston."

"But who would target him?" Vicky asked with growing aggravation. "He had only just arrived. Who would do something so terrible?"

"Well," Mitchell reached up and ruffled his fingers through his hair. "We do have a suspect in mind."

"You do?" Aunt Ida asked as she walked up behind Mitchell. Nicholas had walked off with a uniformed officer to answer some questions about what he might have seen or heard. Vicky was beginning to calm down, knowing that there was a suspect was a very good thing.

"Who is it?" Vicky inquired.

"I can't say," Mitchell said but he glanced over his shoulder as more uniformed officers surrounded Nicholas.

"Nicholas?" Ida asked with surprise as she realised what was happening. "That's not possible. He would never do this. He's not that kind of man."

Mitchell arched an eyebrow and lowered his voice to a respectful tone. "Forgive me Ida, but how long have you known this man to be able to make such an assumption?"

"Long enough," Ida snapped back with confidence. She frowned as Nicholas was led past them to the elevator. "This just isn't possible," she insisted sternly. "Nicholas is a good man."

"And he was also up for the same promotion as Charleston," Vicky pointed out with widening eyes. "After Charleston teased him at the reception desk, he must have been livid. He probably decided to make sure that he was the one to get the promotion."

"Those are all assumptions," Aunt Ida huffed and shook her head. "There is no way that Nicholas did this."

"No one's saying he did," Mitchell replied calmly and met Ida's eyes. "Right now the evidence points in his direction. We just want to find out a little more information from him down at the station," he glanced past Ida to Vicky.

"Are you going to be okay?" he asked her tenderly.

"Yes," Vicky nodded. "I'll be fine, I promise," she insisted when he hesitated to leave her side.

"All right, I'll let you know of any developments, okay?" he glanced between the two and then narrowed his blue eyes slightly. "Even though I don't think that there is any danger to be concerned about, the two of you should be cautious. Call me for any reason."

"We will," Ida assured him and then waved him away. "Now hurry off and release Nicholas, he's obviously innocent."

Mitchell offered Ida a tight smile and then joined the other officers on the elevator. Vicky watched the elevator doors slide shut, and tried not to think too much about what had just happened. She didn't have much time to, before Ida grabbed her firmly by the arm and pulled her into a nearby room.

"Hey..." Vicky started to say as she was pulled slightly off balance. Aunt Ida might have had a slender frame but she was very strong.

"I need to talk to you," Aunt Ida whispered and closed the door behind them.

As soon as they were alone in the room together, Ida spun around to face Vicky. "We have to do something about this," she said sternly.

"Aunt Ida, we need to stay out of this," Vicky argued as she stepped closer to her aunt. "This is a very high profile situation, and it looks to me that Mitchell and his crew have things under control. I don't want to step on your toes, but I would suspect Nicholas as well."

"Of course you would," Aunt Ida growled and threw her hands up into the air. "Don't you see? That's why this is the perfect crime. It was expected that someone would have to take the fall for the murder, what better person to frame than Nicholas?"

"If that's the case then I'm sure Mitchell will figure it out," Vicky pointed out as calmly as she could. "I know that you and Nicholas had a moment..."

"Not just a moment," Ida corrected sharply. "We shared wine together, we talked, I know he's not the one who did this."

"Aunt Ida, just because a man is friendly to you doesn't necessarily mean..." Vicky attempted to inject reason into the conversation, but Aunt Ida cut her off before she could succeed.

"Don't tell me what a man's intentions are Vicky, I know them very well. I also know a good man when I meet one, and Nicholas is just that," she was so determined that she jabbed a finger towards Vicky's face, causing Vicky to raise her eyebrows with surprise and narrowly dodge the offending finger.

"Listen to me, Aunt Ida, if you were with Nicholas then why didn't you tell Mitchell?" Vicky asked with some annoyance. "You could have been his alibi."

Ida pursed her lips and tilted her head to the side as she considered the best way to say what she knew she had to say.

"The problem is that Nicholas did leave the room," Ida reluctantly confessed. "He left for just a few minutes because he thought he had left his wallet in the car."

"And did he?" Vicky pushed gently.

"Honestly, I found it in his suitcase while he was gone," Ida said in a whisper. She knew how this would look to Vicky.

"Aunt Ida, it sounds to me like he was trying to use you as an alibi," Vicky pressed her lips together with annoyance. "Can you recall how long the two of you were alone together?"

"It wasn't very long. I left when you called, he uh," she cleared her throat. "He was very nice to me," she was blushing when she looked back towards Vicky.

"Being nice doesn't make him innocent," Vicky reminded her aunt though she tried to keep her words tender. "He would only need a few minutes to commit the crime," Vicky pointed out and sighed as she smoothed her hands down along her hips. "Aunt Ida, I know that you like this man. But just imagine. What if while he was gone he was taking another man's life? What if sharing wine with you was all an attempt to distract you or create an alibi for himself?" she searched her aunt's eyes intently, hoping that she wasn't hurting her feelings.

"Vicky," Aunt Ida drew a slow breath and then released it just as slowly. "I know the man I met did not do this. He even told me over the wine that he had no expectation of getting the position, and it was just a charade he had to go through for the sake of the CEO, to make it look as if he was choosing fairly."

"Don't you think that might have hurt him more deeply then he was admitting?" Vicky asked tentatively and guided her aunt to the small table in the corner of the room.

"No," Ida said with determination. "I may not be the most grounded person," she pursed her lips and rolled her eyes a little. "But my instincts about people have always been good. He was so caring, and so courteous. I can't even imagine him striking a fly let alone taking a life."

Vicky nodded solemnly. "One thing I've come to learn Aunt Ida, is that sometimes people only show us the side of them they want us to know."

Aunt Ida still shook her head and fluttered her hands in her lap before she finally stood up with a growl.

"No, Vicky. If I'm wrong, the investigation will prove me wrong. But what are the chances that they will even look at other suspects if they already have the perfect suspect?" she frowned.

"Mitchell is smarter than that, Aunt Ida," Vicky said with confidence. "He will get to the bottom of things," then she paused a moment and looked over at her aunt. She usually had a cheerful glow, a confident aura about her. In that moment Aunt Ida looked like a frail woman, lost and alone. It was a side of her aunt that Vicky had never seen before. "But..." she sighed.

"But?" Ida perked up a little bit.

"But, I don't think it could hurt if we poked around, just a little bit," Vicky finally murmured. "Let's wait until Mitchell clears the room, then we'll have a look for ourselves," she suggested. "Until then," she met Ida's eyes intently, "stay away from Nicholas Brendan."

"Vicky, I'm an adult," Ida huffed and shook her head. "If I want to see him..."

"No," Vicky said sternly and then reached out for her aunt's hand. "Please Aunt Ida, you're all Sarah and I have and I can't bear the thought of anything happening to you."

Ida looked as if she might protest, but her expression softened with Vicky's words.

"I promise to be careful," she finally agreed, though she didn't commit to avoiding Nicholas completely.

"Good," Vicky sighed and gave her aunt's hand a light squeeze. "I'm going to go downstairs and see if Mitchell needs anything, plus, I'm going to have to call Sarah," she groaned. She knew her sister would be livid that she hadn't called immediately. "Just stick close to me, or other members of the staff Aunt Ida, I don't want you wandering around alone."

"I'll be fine dear," Aunt Ida assured her and then added. "The same goes for you, you know."

"Yes Ma'am," Vicky grinned and then headed down the stairs to the first floor. She took the stairs because she wanted to avoid the now extremely curious guests. She and Sarah would have to work together to come up with an official announcement. As she dialled her sister on her cell phone and tried to push open the door at the bottom of the stairs that led into the lobby, something suddenly struck her. If she hadn't been able to open the door to get into Charleston's room because his body was blocking it, how had the person on the inside who had committed the crime got out? The thought was pushed out of her mind as she gave the door a hard shove and began filling her sister in on the events of the evening.

"I can't believe this," Sarah gasped into the phone when she heard the news. "I should come in. Are you safe? Do you want to shut down the inn?"

"Mitchell thinks that Charleston was targeted, and this place is crawling with police. I don't think that anything else is going to happen," she pointed out. "So you should stay home. I just wanted to know how you thought I should address this with the clients," she paused a moment before confessing with a grimace. "Jeremy Minkle is threatening to sue."

Through the phone, Vicky heard Sarah take a sharp breath. "Don't do anything," she said swiftly. "Don't say anything to the guests. If you have to talk to any of them, just mention that it's a police matter and it's being handled."

"Are you sure?" Vicky asked as she stepped inside the lobby.

"Yes, we'll make an announcement in the morning. That will give Mitchell some time to investigate, and hopefully the guests will have some time to calm down," Sarah sighed on the other end of the phone. "I'm sorry I wasn't there to help you with this Vicky."

"Sarah it's all right I took care of it," Vicky assured her and already regretted disturbing her.

"Please, please, try to get some rest. We can meet in the restaurant for breakfast tomorrow, okay?"

"I'll be there," Sarah promised and yawned as she hung up the phone.

Chapter Four

When Vicky walked further into the lobby she saw several uniformed officers quietly talking to different guests. Vicky recognized them as all being at the inn for the conference. As she walked closer their muttered comments revealed that she wasn't going to find any sympathy for Nicholas in this group.

"You know I never would have suspected that Brendan could be capable of something like this, but I guess getting passed over one more time just made him snap," one woman said as she shook her head with dismay. "Such a terrible waste."

Vicky pursed her lips and shifted casually towards another conversation, under the guise of straightening up some of the brochures.

"Yeah Brendan could be a bit of a hot head," a man was saying to one of the officers. "One time when we went on a trip to the Keys he got into a fist fight with one of the managers. We all have our moments, but you know throwing punches is just taking things a little too far," the man shrugged and glanced away nervously. Vicky bit her bottom lip as Nicholas was looking more and more guilty. He certainly didn't have very many supporters. She turned around to straighten out some more brochures when she saw Mitchell walking across the lobby towards her. She fanned the brochures guiltily out on the table, knowing that she had been eavesdropping on a police investigation.

"Hello sweetheart," Mitchell said in a murmur beside her ear. He was careful not to be too affectionate in front of the other officers. "I asked them to do the questioning in private, I'm sorry they're out in the lobby."

"It's fine," Vicky said quickly and then added. "Most of the guests that are staying here are here for the conference, so they've all heard about what happened."

"Sorry to say that it's only going to get worse," Mitchell sighed and drew his fingertips across his forehead to ease some tension he was feeling. "The time frame that Nicholas admits to being away from Ida is the exact time frame that the ME estimated the time of death."

Vicky winced at that revelation. She was hoping that the time of death would rule out Nicholas' potential involvement. She listened attentively as Mitchell continued. "Worse, we've still not found the murder weapon, but the ME has given us a guess as to what it was."

"What did she think it was?" Vicky asked, her eyes focusing on him.

"Looks like it was a corkscrew," he admitted.

"Oh no," Vicky replied her voice trembling.

"What?" Mitchell asked and studied her intently.

"I did receive a request from Nicholas to leave a corkscrew in his room, along with some wine," Vicky winced as she admitted this. She knew that Ida would be upset with her, but she had to agree with Mitchell. Every shred of evidence was pointing right at Nicholas.

"I'll send a uniformed officer to see if it's still there," he said. "Do you have a list of what other rooms requested a corkscrew?" he questioned.

"Henry will have it," she replied.

"Can you ask Henry for the list and also a list of where any other corkscrews might be located, please. Then we can collect them and have them evaluated," he made a note in his small notebook and then tucked it back in his pocket.

"I will, right now," Vicky agreed with a frown. "So I'm guessing that Nicholas won't be getting out any time soon?"

"We're holding him for now," Mitchell nodded and then reached up to rub lightly at the back of his neck. He grimaced as he did, and Vicky recognized this as an indication that he was uncomfortable.

"What is it?" Vicky tried to pull more information from him as she studied him.

"It's just," he hesitated a moment. "Nicholas looks perfect for the murder. He's got motive, opportunity, and now potentially the murder weapon. But something doesn't fit. If he really was planning to murder Charleston, why did he wait until they got here? And why not arrive with a more effective weapon than a corkscrew?"

"That's a good point," Vicky tapped her chin lightly as she considered his words. "It seems much more like a crime of passion than a planned assault," as her mind drifted back to the crime scene, she recalled what she had thought of earlier. "One other thing, Mitchell," Vicky added in a lower voice. "Just how did the murderer get out of the room? It took all of my strength to force that door open to get in. So how did he get out?"

"We're looking into that," Mitchell nodded. "Maybe through the window and onto the balcony. The crime techs are evaluating the scene right now."

"I'll go talk to Henry," Vicky nodded. "Let me know if there's anything else you need."

"Oh, be on the lookout for Charleston's fiancée, she's been roaming around here half-drunk and very angry," Mitchell warned. "She hasn't been ruled out as a suspect either Vicky, so please be very careful."

"I am, I promise," Vicky leaned up and pecked his cheek lightly. Mitchell blushed at the kiss and smiled.

Vicky headed for the kitchen, but when she got there she found the door was closed and locked. This didn't surprise her as it was getting late and room service was only offered until certain hours. What did surprise her was that when she looked through the small glass rectangle window in the door, Henry was not inside. He usually spent a little extra time after the kitchen was closed either preparing dishes for the next day, or experimenting with a new recipe. Perhaps all of the police activity had scared him off. If that was the case then Vicky was sure she could find him in the staff quarters.

They offered rooms at very cheap prices to the staff. This partly off-set the cost of their salaries and was also a great benefit for the employees as they had no commuting time. They also had access to all the amenities, such as the pool, the gardens, the kitchen, and the large banquet room. It made the employees of the inn feel more like a family to Vicky and Sarah, than just people on the payroll, and that's how they preferred it. As she walked down the narrow path through the gardens that led to the staffs' quarters she thought once more about the crime scene.

She was certain that there was something she had overlooked in the room. Something had to explain how the murderer had left the room. She was so distracted that she found herself walking to the wrong door. She didn't realize it, until she heard noises coming from inside. She stood frozen with her hand poised to knock on the door as she listened to the unmistakable sounds that were drifting through the thick wooden door. It was moaning, but not of a fearful kind. She could also hear Emily's voice.

"Oh, Jeremy," she moaned.

Vicky's eyes widened at what she was hearing. She tried to convince herself that maybe she was just misinterpreting, but there was no questioning it when she heard further evidence.

She quickly lowered her hand and tried to decide what to do. Emily knew that fraternising with the guests was frowned upon, but they weren't terribly strict about it. People often came to the inn looking for romance, so it wasn't that surprising if they found it with one of the staff members. But this wasn't just any guest, this was Jeremy Minkle, CEO of Ballant Industries, and the man who had threatened to destroy the inn with a lawsuit. She wondered if Emily knew about that. Before she could decide what to do, she heard her name called.

"Vicky, are you looking for me?" Henry asked as he walked towards her. Vicky's eyes grew even wider as she heard the sounds come to an abrupt stop inside of Emily's room. She hurried away from the door and tugged Henry into his room which was right beside Emily's.

"Did you know that Emily was dating Jeremy Minkle?" she asked in a whisper as soon as they were alone.

"Well, how couldn't I?" Henry chuckled as he pointed to the wall. "It's pretty thin, and they're not exactly quiet."

"You should have told me," Vicky chastised and crossed her arms.

"Why?" Henry asked with surprise. "I didn't see any harm in it. Emily's a sweet girl, besides they were together the last time that Jeremy stayed here."

"Oh, really?" Vicky asked with surprise. "No wonder she booked him a room," she nodded. "And it doesn't bother you?"

"Look," Henry shrugged. "She's young, she's a nice girl, and if she ends up marrying the fellow she'll have a very different life. Of course I've tried to warn her that Jeremy Minkle is not the marrying type, but she seems head over heels anyway."

"Hmm," Vicky glanced at the wall. She could hear some scuffling around and guessed that they were hurrying to get dressed. "Well, I was looking for you," she said as she turned back to Henry. "It turns out the murder weapon is more than likely a corkscrew. So we need to make a list of where the corkscrews are for the police."

"Sure, I'll get right on it," Henry agreed, then he hesitated a moment and met Vicky's eyes. "If you decide to talk to Emily, go easy on her, she's really just a sweet kid looking for love."

"I'll be easy," Vicky promised as they stepped out of Henry's room together. Her gaze lingered on the door to Emily's room. She still thought it was strange that she hadn't known about their affair. She usually knew about everything that went on at the inn. So Emily must have done a very good job of hiding it. But why would she? Emily knew Vicky well enough to realize that Vicky wouldn't begrudge her a little romance. As Vicky walked back towards the inn, she saw several police cars pulling away from the parking lot. Mitchell must have sent them home for the night. The guests were likely too tired to offer helpful interviews at this point. She stepped into the lobby to find Mitchell waiting for her.

"Henry has headed to the kitchen to sort out the list," she said quickly as she walked up to him. He spun around and wrapped an arm instantly around her waist.

"I'm sorry we missed our evening," he said with a sigh. "I'll have to get an officer to collect the corkscrews and then get that evidence back to the station."

"I know," Vicky said with a patient smile. "Don't worry, we'll make up for it when we do have time."

"Actually," Mitchell's lips spread wide into a smile that she knew too well. It was his 'I have a secret' smile that drove her wild, as he was incredibly good at keeping secrets. "I am planning on it," he smiled.

"What does that mean?" Vicky asked and studied his expression for any hint.

"I guess we'll just have to make the time to find out," he smiled and kissed her gently. "Go get some rest. I'm going to leave a few uniformed officers to keep an eye on the inn tonight, okay?"

"Okay," Vicky agreed, though she wanted to grill him about the secret that he was keeping. She knew this was not the time. When she reached her apartment she was ready to collapse. She had made sure that both the uniformed officers and the inn's security guard had her cell phone number and instructed them to call if anything came up. She placed her cell phone on the table beside her bed and then fell into it.

Chapter Five

Vicky hadn't been asleep for very long, maybe an hour, when she heard knocking on her door. Sleepily she sat up. She glanced at the clock, and then her cell phone. As she checked to see if anyone had called, she heard another insistent knock, and then her cell phone began to ring.

"Hello?" she said sleepily as she stumbled towards the front door of her apartment.

"Vicky, did I wake you?" Ida asked and the knocking continued.

"No someone at my door..." Vicky began to say until she looked through the small peep hole in her door. "Well, yes, actually you did," she said as she hung up the phone and opened the door. Aunt Ida stood in front of her, her phone still pressed up to her ear.

"We need to talk," she said into the phone.

"Aunt Ida, you can hang up now," Vicky shook her head and set her phone down on the entranceway table as Aunt Ida stepped inside.

"What is this about?" Vicky asked, stifling a yawn.

"I can't sleep, can you?" Aunt Ida said quickly, her eyes wide and dancing nervously from place to place in the apartment.

"Yes, actually," Vicky said, and then reminded herself to be patient. "How much coffee have you had?" she asked as she studied her aunt.

"Enough," Aunt Ida shrugged. "I saw that the police were gone, and I thought maybe we could take a look at the crime scene."

"It's the middle of the night, Aunt Ida!" Vicky said with a frown.

"Which is the perfect time," Aunt Ida reminded her. "If Mitchell sees us looking through the room tomorrow he's going to kick us out, and you know it."

"Good point," Vicky nodded slightly in agreement. She preferred not to argue with Mitchell if at all possible. That did mean that if they were going to look through the crime scene, it would have to be at night.

"Are there any officers posted at the door?" Vicky asked as she walked back towards her bedroom to grab some fresh clothes.

"Not that I saw," Ida replied as she sat down on the couch. "I just can't stop thinking about poor Nicholas sitting in a jail cell. How can they still be holding him?"

"Well, they haven't arrested him yet, not officially," Vicky explained as she pulled on a new shirt and tucked a flashlight into her back pocket. "But they can hold him for twenty-four hours for questioning. After that they have to release or arrest him."

"Oh, that's a relief," Aunt Ida said. "At least he'll be out of there by tomorrow night."

When Vicky stepped back into the living room she couldn't hide her frown.

"What?" Aunt Ida asked when she saw Vicky's expression.

"With the evidence they have it's very likely that they will arrest Nicholas," Vicky explained as gently as she could. "He has no alibi, he has a motive, and he did have a corkscrew in his room."

"A corkscrew?" Ida asked with surprise. "What does that have to do with anything?"

"Well, the ME believes that is what was used as the murder weapon," Vicky sat down beside her aunt and enveloped her hand with her own. "Try not to be too upset. You know that if he's not guilty, Mitchell will figure it out."

"Do I?" Aunt Ida asked in a testy tone of voice. "If everyone believes he's guilty, and I'm the only one who thinks he is innocent, then how do I know that?"

Vicky hugged her aunt and nodded. She looked directly into her eyes. "Then we'll make sure he has all the information that he needs to discover the truth. Okay?"

"You must think I'm very silly," Aunt Ida fretted as she glanced away from Vicky.

"I don't," Vicky insisted, but her aunt was not convinced.

"I know that I've just met him, and I should trust Mitchell's judgement, but this man, there's just so much honesty in him. He even told me about his late wife. I just don't think he has the heart of a cold blooded killer, and for an innocent man to spend the rest of his life in jail is a horrible thought."

"I understand," Vicky murmured as Ida's words settled in. She hadn't really looked at things from Nicholas' perspective. If he really was innocent, then he had to be terrified. "Let's go take a look at the crime scene," Vicky said as she stood up and headed for the door. Ida followed after her. The pair walked quietly through the lobby. Vicky was hoping to avoid the security guard and the police officers that Mitchell had asked to stay the night. She pushed the button and hoped the elevator would move quickly. As soon as the doors opened she guided Ida inside and pushed the button for the third floor. When Vicky noticed Aunt Ida's determined stare in the reflection of the metal doors she frowned.

"Aunt Ida, I don't want you to get your hopes up," Vicky warned. "The police did a thorough search, there may be nothing new to find."

"We'll find something," Aunt Ida said with confidence. "It's just a matter of looking in the right places."

Vicky gritted her teeth and nodded. When the elevator doors slid open she checked the hall to make sure no one was there. Then she and Ida made their way into Charleston's room. Once they had slipped in Vicky flipped on her flashlight. She didn't want to turn on the light in the room as it might draw too much attention.

"Look at this mess," Aunt Ida fussed as there was fingerprint dust all over the room.

Vicky decided to search the room. She started at one corner and made her way across the back wall, looking closely for any small trace of evidence. When she reached the windowsill, she remembered what Mitchell had said about the possibility that the murderer had gone out the window.

Vicky studied the windowsill. The windowsill wasn't splintered or damaged in any way. It seemed very odd to her to think that someone might have climbed out of the window without leaving behind even the slightest scuff mark and where would they have gone, the room was three floors up. But that had to be the case, didn't it? When she had opened the door to the room, she was forced to shove Charleston's body in order to do so. So how could anyone have walked out of the room without disturbing the body laying in front of the door?

"It just doesn't make any sense," Vicky pointed out. As she swept her gaze over the scene for what felt like the thousandth time, she was beginning to feel like Mitchell. "There is no way that someone could kill Charleston and then climb over him to get out the door," Vicky was completely puzzled.

"Maybe he was still alive," Aunt Ida suggested thoughtfully. "Maybe he crawled to the door after the murderer left."

Vicky considered this for a moment as she looked at the pattern of the bloodstains on the floor.

"But there's no trail leading to the door," she pointed out. "Everything is pooled right around and under the door," Vicky walked towards the door, inspecting the carpet as she did. She tried to imagine what had happened inside the room. Had he known his assailant? The door hadn't been forced open, so he must have opened the door for the person to enter. It was impossible to tell for sure since there was very little physical evidence. The room was not tossed, there was nothing missing, and it was clear that the main target was Charleston himself.

"This is so frustrating," Aunt Ida growled as she looked around the room. "There must be something here! Maybe we are missing something because this room is so big."

"That's it!" Vicky gasped as a childhood memory returned.

"What?" Aunt Ida questioned with confusion.

But Vicky didn't reply, she just started searching the wall.

"What are you doing?" Aunt Ida asked again with a quizzical look. But, before Vicky could answer she noticed a piece of moulding at the base of the wall missing. She pushed at the section and the wall dipped inward. Aunt Ida and Vicky stared in shock.

"Aunt Ida, do you see what I'm seeing?" Vicky asked as she shone her flashlight into the dark space beyond the hidden door.

"I think so," Aunt Ida tilted her head to the side. "But I don't know what we're looking at exactly."

"I think it used to be the passageway that led form the storeroom to the old laundry," Vicky gasped and poked her head inside. She had a faint memory of running along a corridor with Sarah when they were kids. It led from an old storeroom upstairs to the old laundry room downstairs. It was designed to be a quick way to get the heavy laundry from the upstairs rooms to the laundry room but when her parents did a small renovation and installed lifts they closed off the passageway and made the storeroom join the adjacent room to make a big guest room. They also moved the laundry room indoors.

"I thought it was completely closed off years ago!" Aunt Ida exclaimed.

As Vicky looked closer, she played the flashlight beam along the floor. She noticed right away a pattern of shoeprints in the thick layer of dust.

"Someone has been here," she said breathlessly. Her heart began to race as she suddenly realized that the person who had left those shoeprints behind, had probably been Charleston's murderer.

"We should follow them," Aunt Ida stated.

Vicky hesitated for a moment before entering the tunnel. She knew that she should tell Mitchell about what they had found. He would want to investigate it, and have the techs check for any evidence left behind. But it was so tempting to head down the passageway. If they didn't look now, then whoever the murderer was might decide to clean up his or her tracks, and in that case all the evidence would be lost.

"Wait, let me take a few pictures," Vicky said quickly and pulled out her phone. She snapped photographs of the shoeprints, and the surrounding walls. The passageway wasn't very wide, it was just big enough for a long, narrow, trolley. She and Ida would have to walk single file. There was nothing she could see on the walls themselves, but Vicky knew that crime scene techs could find things that were invisible to the naked eye.

Vicky stepped in first. She did her best not to disturb the shoeprints that were in the dust, but she knew she was creating new ones of her own. Then Aunt Ida followed after her. Vicky held her flashlight out in front of her and shone it down the passageway.

"I can't believe you can still access this," she muttered as she shook her head. "Stay close to me, I have no idea how strong these floors are or how many spiders..." she realized her mistakes the moment she said the word.

"Spiders?" Aunt Ida gasped and Vicky glanced over her shoulder sharply.

"Shh," she warned her aunt, as she knew that Aunt Ida could begin shrieking very loudly when spiders were involved. "I'm sure if there were any, they were scared off by whoever walked through here," as she turned back around she cringed, hoping that her words would turn out to be true. In the beam of light that the flashlight cast she noticed that the shoeprints seemed to be even and large. She assumed that they would have come from a man. But who? She wasn't certain of that. At least they didn't have heel marks, indicating that the criminal they were seeking was not likely Amanda. The passageway abruptly curved and sloped downwards.

"Where does this come out?" Aunt Ida asked.

"I don't know, I thought they closed this off. The outside laundry room no longer exists," Vicky whispered back. She had tried to keep her bearings as to where they would be in the inn, but she had lost track when the corridor began to slope. She shone her flashlight ahead of her and saw that the passageway came to an abrupt end. All that was in front of her were stones, maybe they only blocked off this end.

"We should go back," Vicky suddenly said, her breath catching in her throat. But as she started to turn back, she caught a flash along the corridor wall. Someone carrying a flashlight was coming. "Aunt Ida," she gasped out as quietly as she could. "Come close to me," she said quickly and flicked off her flashlight.

Aunt Ida huddled close to Vicky and the two women held their breath as they heard footsteps slowly approaching. Vicky leaned her shoulder against the side wall as the passageway was still very narrow. She felt her shoulder strike something protruding from the wall. Suddenly she was falling through the wall, and pulling Aunt Ida down with her. She landed hard on the floor, and Aunt Ida landed rather softly right on top of her. Vicky helped her aunt up to her feet and fearfully looked in the direction of the tunnel. The hidden door that had swung open when she depressed the lever for it, had swung back closed.

"Where are we?" Aunt Ida asked with some confusion as she looked around the small room. It was familiar, but not one of the guest rooms at the inn. Then Vicky noticed the framed painting hanging on the wall. It was of a vase of carnations that Vicky knew Emily had painted.

Vicky cupped her hand over her mouth to keep from gasping out loud. When she composed herself she whispered to her aunt. "We're in Emily's room."

"Emily?" Aunt Ida said with surprise. Just then they heard footsteps from the wall. Whoever had been following them had reached the end of the corridor. Vicky waved frantically towards the closet. She and Ida crept as silently as they could into the closet and closed themselves inside. They both waited to see who would come through the opening in the wall. But no one did. Minutes passed by, and nothing happened.

"Maybe the person didn't know the door was there?" Vicky whispered to her aunt.

"But how could he not know, if he's the killer?" Aunt Ida pointed out with mounting frustration. Vicky was just about to open the closet door when the door to Emily's room swung open. Emily walked inside and sat down on the foot of her bed. She looked morose as she stared hard at the floor. She reached up and released her blonde curls. As her hair tumbled around her shoulders, Vicky peered through the slats of the closet.

"There you are," a voice said from the doorway with annoyance. "I've been looking everywhere for you."

"What do you want, Henry?" Emily asked brusquely. She didn't usually talk to anyone that way.

"I just wanted to see if you were okay," Henry explained in a hurt tone. "I heard you two arguing..."

"You didn't hear anything," Emily snapped and glared at Henry.

"But I did..." Henry began to say again.

"You didn't," Emily shot back. "We were just role-playing."

"Role-playing?" Henry replied with a shake of his head. "I don't think so. I heard you crying. Then when I came over, you were gone. Look Emily, I'm not trying to get into your business, but you should know that you don't have to put up with that kind of treatment."

All of the fire and fury seemed to drain right out of Emily and she began to quietly cry. Vicky had to fight the urge to go to her and comfort her, as she knew that there was no way they could explain hiding in her closet.

Henry sat down beside her and patted her back gently. "It's okay hon, let it all out."

Emily gulped and shook her head. "It's nothing. I just expected too much, that's all."

"Shh," Henry soothed her. "Why don't we go hit up the freezer for some of that gourmet ice cream?"

"But won't Vicky or Sarah be mad?" Emily asked nervously.

"What they don't know won't hurt them," Henry said conspiratorially. Vicky narrowed her green eyes sharply and bit into her bottom lip to keep from correcting that statement. Instead she felt Aunt Ida squeeze her hand firmly. As Henry and Emily left the room, Vicky let out a sigh of relief. She opened up the closet door so that she and Aunt Ida could have some breathing room. As they stepped out of the closet, Vicky stepped down on something hard. She glanced down to see a pillowcase, wrapped up several times into a small bundle that had been shoved into the bottom of the closet.

"What's this?" she murmured as she crouched down to peer at it.

"Just looks like some dirty laundry," Aunt Ida shrugged as she glanced nervously around the room. "We should get out of here before they, or the guy from the corridor comes back."

Vicky nodded, but she was distracted by the pillowcase. "There was something hard inside it when I stepped down," Vicky said quietly. She reached out and picked up the pillowcase. When she unwound it, she revealed a corkscrew with a long wooden handle.

"Aunt Ida?" she breathed as she turned around to show her the corkscrew. She was careful not to touch anything but the pillowcase.

"Do you think that's it?" Aunt Ida looked at the corkscrew with horror. Vicky immediately began wrapping the corkscrew back up. She tucked it back into the closet where she found it.

"We have to let Mitchell know about this," she said quickly. "All of this."

"But first we need to get out of here," Ida said quickly. "We don't want to be next on the list." Vicky dialled Mitchell as they left Emily's room. When he answered, she hesitated.

"Vicky?" Mitchell pressed, waiting to hear why she had called.

"Mitchell, Aunt Ida and I found a hidden passage," Vicky said haltingly.

"A what?" Mitchell asked, both surprise and alarm changing his tone.

"I thought my parents had it closed off years ago. It leads from the room where

Charleston was killed, to the staff quarters," she explained, though she was still hesitant. She really liked Emily. She couldn't see her as a killer. Not only that but the shoeprints in the passageway had been very large. She was certain they were not Emily's.

"Vicky, I have to tell you something, I've been calling for ten minutes," he added with annoyance. Vicky had turned her phone to silent. It was a good thing she had, considering that they had just stepped out of the closet they were hiding in. She was so busy listening to Mitchell, that she didn't notice the person walking up to them, until she heard Aunt Ida gasp.

"Uh," Vicky stared at Nicholas, who was standing right in front of both of them. "Is it that you released Nicholas Brendan?" Vicky whispered into the phone.

"We had to," Mitchell replied with a sigh. "He had a very expensive lawyer, and we didn't have any DNA evidence to hold him on. The corkscrew in his room came back clear, but it could have been wiped clean."

Vicky was holding tightly to her cell phone. Did that mean that it had been Nicholas that followed them down the passageway? But why would he need to sneak into Emily's room? All of a sudden, it all made sense.

"You did this, didn't you?" she asked as she widened her eyes.

"Vicky, who are you talking to?" Mitchell asked.

"Vicky, don't say that," Aunt Ida insisted.

Nicholas only blinked. "I'm sorry if I startled you. I was looking for the two of you. The security guard said that you were in Charleston's room. But when I went there, you weren't there," he explained.

"You would know where we were," Vicky said calmly. "Because, you followed us down the same hidden passageway that you used to plant this evidence in Emily's room."

"What evidence?" Mitchell asked on the phone. "Vicky, I'm coming over there right now."

Vicky hung up the phone and continued to glower at Nicholas. He looked as if he was going to attempt to defend himself, but instead he sighed with defeat.

"All right, it's true," he shook his head.

"What's true?" Aunt Ida asked with apprehension.

"I did follow the two of you down the passageway," he admitted and ran his fingertips along his forehead, and back over the area that was receding.

"Oh no Nicholas, it can't be true," Ida gasped out as she looked at him.

"It is true," he said grimly. "I did follow the two of you. The door was partially open, and when I looked inside I saw a flashlight beam. I was worried that somehow you'd been hurt. So I followed you."

Aunt Ida smiled with relief. "So you didn't know the passageway was there before hand?"

"Of course not," Nicholas insisted with frustration. "I didn't do this. I didn't hurt Charleston, and I didn't plant any evidence," he added as he looked over at Vicky. "In fact, I don't even know where you two went. When I reached the end of the passageway there was no way out. How did you get out of there?"

Aunt Ida was about to tell him when Vicky laid her hand lightly on her aunt's shoulder.

"Don't," she warned her. "We need to find out who did know about the passage, it's better if Nicholas knows nothing about it at all."

"Why do you say that?" Nicholas asked quizzically as he studied her. "Don't you think I'm guilty?"

"No," Vicky suddenly said and shook her head. "No, I don't Nicholas. I don't think you had anything to do with this. I'm sorry if I made you feel that I did."

Nicholas studied her, as if he was trying to figure out whether to believe her or not.

"It's okay, Nicholas," Aunt Ida reassured him. "If Vicky believes your innocent that means she'll do everything in her power to prove it."

"Yes, I will," Vicky agreed.

"You will?" Mitchell questioned as he jogged up to the small gathering. "What's going on here?" he demanded as he looked between Aunt Ida, Nicholas, and Vicky.

"How did you get here so fast?" Vicky asked as she looked from him to the parking lot. Mitchell shifted awkwardly and then lowered his voice.

"Once we released Nicholas, I wanted to make sure you were okay," he murmured. "So I might have been camping out in the parking lot."

"Might have been?" Vicky arched an eyebrow.

Mitchell drew his lips into a thin line of warning. She knew that he had a job to do, and he needed to focus on it.

"I want all of you to tell me everything you know, now please," Mitchell said sternly as he flipped open his notebook.

Vicky described remembering and then finding the passageway, and showed him the shoeprints she had taken pictures of. Then she took Mitchell aside and confessed to hiding in Emily's closet and finding what she believed to be the murder weapon.

"I know that you need a search warrant," Vicky explained. "That's why I left it right where it was. I didn't touch the handle or the metal part at all," she insisted when she saw his disapproving expression.

"Vicky, I care about the evidence, but I also care about you," he reminded her. "If Emily had something to do with this, then you were in danger the entire time you were in her room. You should have called me the moment you found the passageway."

"Well, maybe if you had told me that you were hanging out in the parking lot I would have," Vicky pointed out with a small smile.

"Good point," Mitchell smiled a little, too. He glanced down at the notepad he was holding and then back up at the room they were standing in front of. "I highly doubt it was Emily who actually committed the murder," he said and clenched his jaw. "Something does not make sense here."

Vicky had her suspicions but she was not ready to share them with Mitchell. She had already assumed that one man, whom she was now convinced was innocent, might be guilty. She didn't want to make the same mistake twice.

"Do you know where Emily is now?" Mitchell asked Vicky.

"Actually I do," she replied with raised eyebrows. She led Mitchell towards the kitchen while Aunt Ida hung back with Nicholas to discuss what they had both seen in the passageway.

"Do you think she's okay with him?" Mitchell asked as Vicky unlocked the side door into the kitchen.

"I think so," Vicky nodded as she glanced over her shoulder just in time to see Aunt Ida embrace Nicholas warmly. Despite the tension of the situation she found herself smiling at the sight.

Chapter Six

When Mitchell and Vicky walked into the kitchen, Henry and Emily looked up guiltily from their bowls of ice cream that were next to a huge bucket of ice cream.

"Vicky, I can explain," Henry said quickly.

"Henry, give us a moment alone please," Vicky said in a stern tone as she settled her gaze on Emily. Mitchell had asked Vicky to stay with him because he thought it would make Emily feel more at ease.

"Sure," Henry nodded and glanced nervously at Emily. "But I swear it was my idea..."

"This is a police matter, Henry," Mitchell explained and gestured towards the door. Henry didn't have to be told again. He headed for the door and glanced sympathetically at Emily as he stepped outside into the garden.

"A police matter?" Emily asked as she looked between Vicky and Mitchell. "Have I done something wrong?"

"Have you?" Vicky challenged, which drew a reproachful look from Mitchell. Vicky cleared her throat and stepped aside, knowing that she had to let Mitchell perform the interrogation. Instead of questioning Emily though, he picked up a bowl and a spoon from the butcher's block that the ice cream container was resting on.

"Do you mind?" he asked as he gestured to the ice cream and met Emily's eyes.

"No, it's fine," Emily replied, though she seemed very confused. Vicky was also confused, she had no idea why Mitchell wanted to eat ice cream instead of talking about the corkscrew she had found.

"How are things going, Emily?" he asked as he dished up some ice cream. When he ate a spoonful he grinned and moaned a little, "Oh, that's tasty."

"Things are going okay I guess," Emily replied. The normally shy girl seemed to be relaxing a little bit.

"That's good," Mitchell nodded as he put the spoon down. "You know, Emily, you've been such a great help over the years to Vicky and Sarah. Vicky's told me so much about you."

"Oh?" Emily blushed a little and glanced at Vicky. Vicky managed a smile in return. The truth was she did often talk about Emily. She had started at the inn when she was only eighteen and was one of the hardest working young women she knew. She always made sure all of her tasks were complete and would often offer to help others that may have fallen behind. She was certainly not someone who would strike her as violent. She seemed to genuinely care about the guests that stayed at the inn and was especially good with the children who stayed there. But, none of that changed what Vicky had found in her closet.

"But it seems to me every time I see you, you're alone," Mitchell suddenly said, drawing Emily's attention sharply back to him.

"Well, I am alone a lot," Emily agreed nervously.

"Shy right?" Mitchell's smile spread warmly. "You know when I was in high school I could barely speak to a girl. If one tried to talk to me, I'd drop my books, stumble over my words, or do something else terribly embarrassing. It got to where I would just avoid them."

Vicky raised an eyebrow. She didn't know this about Mitchell, and wondered if he was telling the truth or just trying to coax Emily. What she couldn't figure out was what he was trying to coax her into.

"I was really shy in school, too," Emily admitted and then she added in a whisper. "I used to snort every time someone tried to talk to me. I couldn't help it!"

"Of course not, some people are just shy," Mitchell shrugged and encouraged her to take another bite of the ice cream.

"But that's changed for me now," Mitchell added. "Since I met Vicky, I don't think I've stuttered over my words once," he glanced up at Vicky with a smile. Vicky was feeling very out of the loop but she smiled at him in return. She was sure he had a plan, but she felt as if he was wasting time. She was more of a charge in and interrogate kind of woman, and though she respected Mitchell's expertise, she was getting impatient.

"Oh me, too," Emily abruptly squealed. "Isn't it amazing when you finally meet the right person?" she asked with a heavy sigh. "It's like all that shyness, all that nervousness just disappears."

"Mmhm," Mitchell agreed and then settled his gaze on her. "So you've met someone like that?"

Suddenly, Vicky knew where Mitchell was going with his line of questioning. So far she hadn't revealed to him that Emily and Jeremy were having an affair. She didn't want to give Jeremy more ammunition for his lawsuit, and she also didn't think it would be relevant. But things had certainly changed.

"Maybe," Emily said more quietly. She seemed to begin to realize that she was getting caught in a trap.

"It must be so hard, someone as beautiful..." he glanced up at Vicky briefly with an apologetic look before looking back at Emily, "as you are, to have to see someone like Amanda with the man you love."

"What?" Emily asked, her eyes widening. "What are you talking about?"

"It's okay, Emily," Mitchell said calmly. "We know what really happened."

"What do you mean?" she demanded.

"Maybe you were hoping that he would leave her for you. Maybe the two of you argued, and you just couldn't help yourself. I know what it's like to feel like things are one-sided, it's like getting slapped across the face."

Vicky stepped closer to the butcher's block. She tried to meet Mitchell's eyes, but he was too busy holding Emily's gaze.

"Did you see Amanda with Charleston? Is that what got you so upset?" he asked with quiet confidence.

"Charleston?" Emily shuddered at that very idea. "You think I was in love with that slob? Please, he's nothing like Jeremy." After she said his name, she reached up and cupped her mouth with her hand. She stared wide eyed at Mitchell, and then looked over at Vicky.

"Jeremy?" Mitchell repeated. It was obvious that he had been in the dark on that one.

"Jeremy Minkle," Vicky supplied, "the CEO of Ballant Industries. He and Emily have been having an affair."

Mitchell shot a cool look at her, and she knew that he was wondering how long she had known about that.

"I'm sorry, Vicky," Emily said quickly. "It just happened last time he was here, and then..."

"And then when he came back, it picked right back up?" Vicky suggested and then shook her head. "Emily, we just want to figure out what happened here. Just be honest with Mitchell."

"I'm trying," Emily promised, she was now very flustered.

"What do you know about Charleston's death?" Mitchell asked pointedly. He was taking advantage of her being a little off balance.

"Nothing," Emily said swiftly. "Nothing at all. I'm telling you, nothing," she insisted.

Mitchell narrowed his eyes and pulled out his notebook, he jotted something down on it and then looked back up at Emily.

"If you know nothing, then you'd be okay with me taking a look around your room?" he asked calmly.

"Of course you can," she shrugged a little and lowered her eyes. "There's nothing for me to hide anymore."

Vicky was surprised by this. She knew what was in Emily's closet. She was certain that it was the murder weapon. So why would she be so comfortable with Mitchell looking in her room? Before she could think about it for too long Mitchell was standing up.

"Let's get that ice cream in the freezer, and go have a look around," he suggested. His tone was still friendly enough that Emily willingly agreed.

"I'll take care of the ice cream," Vicky volunteered.

She needed a moment alone to try to piece together the puzzle. Mitchell nodded and led

Emily out to her room. Vicky already knew what he would find in her closet. She also knew that it might lead to Emily's arrest. But she was sure that Emily had not committed the crime. What motive could she have to kill Charleston? She didn't seem to have the strength to kill him with a corkscrew. She knew something wasn't quite right. She took the time to sort through all of the information she had swimming through her mind.

Everything led back to one name. It didn't make sense to her, but it did lead back to only one name. It was a hunch she decided to investigate on her own.

Chapter Seven

Vicky rode the elevator up to the third floor. It was very quiet in the hallway, the sun had not even risen yet. The guests had not begun to wake up. But when she paused beside one door in particular she heard footsteps. Slow, deliberate footsteps. Vicky narrowed her eyes. She considered knocking on the door, but the knob began to turn before she could.

Vicky didn't want to be caught off guard so she ducked into the shadows of the hallway. It was still dim enough that the focus of her hunch did not notice her. She hoped he would get into the elevator. It would give her a chance to search his room. Instead he paused in front of Charleston's room. He stared into the open doorway, and then he spoke, causing a shiver to race along Vicky's spine.

"Why did you want to see me?" he asked. Vicky was about to assume he was talking to a ghost, when she heard another voice reply.

"You know exactly why I wanted to see you," Amanda said with a growl. "Just because Charleston's dead doesn't mean that our deal doesn't still apply."

"You can't be serious," he scoffed and shook his head. "Let's talk about this," he suggested and stepped into the room. Vicky's heart was racing. She had suspected that it wasn't Emily who had committed the crime, but someone she was willing to protect. Someone like Jeremy Minkle. Watching him disappear into the very room where Charleston was killed, but this time with Amanda, made Vicky very uneasy. She crept up to the door to listen in.

"Amanda, you don't want to toy with me," Jeremy said with that confident arrogance.

"I'm not toying," Amanda shot back sharply. "Charleston blew his money as fast as it came in, he was counting on that CEO position. I won't even get his properties because we weren't married. I want the money you were going to give him. I won't say a word if you just give me the money."

"What words will you say if I don't?" Jeremy asked gruffly, Vicky could tell that he had moved closer to Amanda by the volume of his voice.

"I'll tell them all about you," Amanda threatened. "I'll tell the police that you're the one that killed Charleston, and why."

"And you think they'll believe you?" he growled. "I'm a very powerful man. There is nothing that is going to stop me from retiring and living a life of luxury. You, you're just a gold digger, they'll see right through you."

"Really?" Amanda countered. "Are they going to see through your little girlfriend, too? Weak Jeremy. You picked someone like that to waste your time with? You could have had someone like me."

"The last thing I would ever want is someone like you," he nearly shouted, then Vicky heard something slam against the wall. She couldn't wait any longer. She knew that whatever dirt she had on Jeremy he was willing to kill to cover up, he had already done it once after all.

Without thinking too much about the danger she was about to put herself in Vicky opened the door to the room. She caught Jeremy with Amanda pressed against the wall. When Jeremy glanced back to see who had opened the door, his eyes were full of rage.

"Get out of here. Can't you see we're having an intimate moment?" he demanded.

"Doesn't look too intimate to me," Vicky countered and met Jeremy's eyes directly. He was trying to figure out how much she knew. She was trying to figure out how to get his hands off Amanda's throat.

"All right, all right," he nodded a little and released Amanda. "I think I've had too much to drink. Right Amanda?" he asked as he shot her a glare.

"Yeah," Amanda rubbed at her neck which was already bruising. "He had far too much to drink."

Nervously, Amanda walked past Jeremy, who looked like he'd rather grab her again then let her go, but he didn't want to risk it in front of

Vicky. Vicky waited until Amanda was safely out of the room, and then was about to follow her, when Jeremy slammed the door shut by leaning forward from behind her. She stared at the suddenly closed door and drew a sharp breath.

"You know, I warned you about my lawyer," he murmured beside her ear as she stood frozen. "Now, do I need to warn you about anything else?"

"Did you give Charleston a warning?" Vicky asked as she turned around to face him. He was towering over her, one hand still placed firmly on the door.

"Charleston wanted to meddle in my future, in my retirement plans," Jeremy explained. "I was going to make him CEO, set him up for life, but that wasn't enough for him. He and his greedy fiancée wanted more. They wanted everything I had saved up to live out my life in luxury, now why would I give that to them?"

"Because they had something on you," Vicky replied, her heart racing. She knew that if Jeremy was willing to tell her so much, then he had no intention of letting her out of that room alive. "What was it Jeremy?" she pressed. "Were you hiding some dark secret?"

Jeremy sighed and rolled his eyes. "It takes a lot of money to get where I am. More than I've ever had. So I borrowed some from the company, just to give myself a little cushion. I didn't want to have to work until I was dead. But, when I wanted to retire too early, Charleston got suspicious. He started looking into my finances, the company's finances, and one day he just walked into my office, plops the proof down on my desk, and declares that he owns me."

Jeremy balled his free hand into a fist. "No one owns me," he said sternly. "But I'm a reasonable man," he added, his tone softening. "I made him an offer, he could take over my position, no questions asked, he could keep pilfering some extra money off the top and set himself up for a luxurious life, too. At first, he was fine with it," Jeremy admitted. "But then suddenly he wants more. I think it was Amanda that put the idea in his head. So, he asked for too much. He paid the price," Jeremy shrugged a little.

"But how?" Vicky asked, trying to prolong their conversation. "How did you get in here to kill Charleston? How did you have an alibi?"

"You don't even know your own inn, do you?" he chuckled. Suddenly they heard voices out in the hall. Vicky didn't have time to try to figure out who they were as Jeremy grabbed her harshly by the arm and thrust her towards the wall. Instead of slamming into the wall however, he nudged the portion of the moulding that opened up the hidden door, and flung her inside. Then he jumped inside with her, and closed the door behind him. He lunged towards Vicky, and she knew this was her last chance to escape. She began to run down the corridor. As she ran she banged on the wall, hoping to get someone's attention. But she knew that everyone was sleeping, and the security and police officers would never hear her.

She was terrified as she heard his pounding footsteps behind her. She recalled the way his hands had been around Amanda's throat, and knew that she would be next. As she neared the end of the corridor she hoped she would be able to get into Emily's room. Maybe Mitchell and Emily would still be there. But Jeremy was gaining on her, and she couldn't get her feet to move any faster. She wished then that she had been a little more cautious, but it was too late for that. She knew that Jeremy had everything to lose if he allowed her to survive. As she neared the doorway that would open into Emily's room, she had no idea where the lever was to open it. She had found it by accident the last time, and she wasn't having that same luck this time.

"This is it," Jeremy said as he slowed down, knowing that she was trapped. "When I stayed here last year, Emily showed this place to me. She made sure the room it opened into was empty so that she could use the passageway. One day I caught her coming through the wall. We shared the secret then. I had no idea how useful it would become to me," he grinned. "Sometimes things just work out for the best," he added as he withdrew a short but sharp knife from his pocket. Vicky opened her mouth to scream, but Jeremy placed his hand over her lips to silence her.

"These walls are pretty thin," he mumbled and placed the blade against her neck. Vicky swung at his hands and tried to knee him in the stomach, but Jeremy was solid. He didn't seem to be bothered by her attempts.

"It's nothing personal, Vicky," he said quietly. "Perhaps you shouldn't have been so nosy."

Vicky felt the sharp edge of the blade beginning to prick her skin as he moved it, but before he could continue, the door to Emily's room swung open. A large picture frame came crashing down on top of Jeremy's head, followed by a swift kick to his wrist to dislodge his grip on the knife. Vicky gasped greedily for air as his hand fell away from her mouth. She heard the knife clatter to the floor. She turned to see Aunt Ida standing in the doorway, her hands on her hips, her eyes narrowed and damning.

"Oh, you messed with the wrong family, honey," she said flatly and pulled back her foot to kick him again.

"Ida," Mitchell said from behind her and pushed past her. He had his gun drawn and trained on the man who was sprawled out on the floor of the corridor.

"Sorry about killing the carnations," Aunt Ida said to Emily as she looked at the damaged painting on the floor next to Jeremy.

"Oh no, Jeremy!" Emily gasped, and covered her mouth with both hands. She was too upset to hear Ida's apology. She looked horrified. But when she saw the dribble of blood on Vicky's neck, her expression changed. "He tried to kill you?" Emily cried out in horror.

"He's not the man you thought he was, Emily," Mitchell said after cuffing Jeremy securely and checking him for weapons. "Look in the bottom of your closet."

Emily walked over to her closet and looked inside. When she saw the rolled up pillowcase she picked it up. Inside she found the corkscrew.

"He put this here?" she murmured quietly. "He was going to set me up."

"He tried with Nicholas at first," Aunt Ida explained. "But then he thought why not let you take the fall?"

Emily's eyes filled with tears as she hurried over to Vicky. She dabbed at her neck with a tissue she had snatched from the box on her bedside table.

"I'm so sorry, Vicky," she said quickly. "I didn't know, I swear."

"You knew enough not to tell Mitchell what really happened," Vicky reminded her. "How did you ever get involved in all of this?"

Emily sighed as she passed a worried look in Mitchell's direction. She knew that she might suffer some serious consequences. Vicky sat down at the end of her bed and patted the space beside her, while Mitchell looked on.

"It's time to tell the truth, Emily," she said firmly. "This isn't a simple matter, a man has died and another man is going to jail."

Jeremy was still out cold from the picture frame to his head, and Mitchell had called paramedics to have him evaluated before they transported him to jail.

"How much did you know about what was going on with Jeremy?" Vicky tried to persuade Emily to speak without giving her too much information.

"We had a bit of a fling, the last time he was here," she explained shyly, her cheeks so red that they resembled tomatoes. "He pursued me, and by the time he left he had me convinced that he truly liked me. About a week ago he called to let me know that he was coming back. He wanted to see me, and he asked me to make sure he had his favorite room booked. I did what he asked," she sighed and shook her head. "Everything seemed fine until Charleston turned up dead. I knew, from how his body was blocking the door, that someone must have used the passageway to do it. I was sure only Jeremy and I knew about it, but I rationalized that maybe someone else knew about it, too."

"But you knew better," Vicky supplied and met the young girl's eyes. "You knew what he had done."

"I didn't know for sure," she insisted. "But when I confronted him about it earlier tonight, he admitted it. He explained the situation, told me that if he hadn't taken care of it, they would have ruined his life. I didn't agree with it," she said quickly. "But the deed had already been done, and," she hesitated for a moment.

"He scared you?" Vicky suggested. It was easy to see how Jeremy could do that, he had terrified her as he chased her through the passageway.

"I was concerned that if I told the truth he might try to kill me, too," she laughed darkly as she glowered in the direction of her closet. "Turns out he had other plans for me."

"I'm sorry, Emily," Vicky said gingerly. "You didn't deserve to go through all of this."

Mitchell, who had been silently listening for most of the conversation, stepped up beside Emily.

"Are you willing to come down to the station and make a statement?" he asked her calmly.

"Yes," she nodded nervously. "It's what I should have done the first moment I suspected that Jeremy was guilty."

Once the paramedics had checked out Jeremy and woken him with smelling salts, he was led out to a waiting police car. He scowled at Vicky and Aunt Ida as he walked past them.

"Nothing's changed. My lawyer will get me out of this, and I will still end up destroying this place," he threatened and struggled against his handcuffs.

Ida and Vicky stared back at him with hardened glares. Neither even batted an eyelid. Jeremy grunted as he was pushed along the pathway. The sun was just beginning to rise, and its light was sparkling on the leaves in the garden.

"Are you ok?" Mitchell asked with concern. "I was worried about you."

"I'll be fine," Vicky replied with a sigh.

"I'm going to take Emily down to the station now," Mitchell said to Vicky quietly. "We'll talk about your little excursion, later, hmm?" he met her gaze with a quirked brow.

"How about we talk about those plans instead?" Vicky suggested as she accepted a bandage from one of the paramedics. The cut on her neck was barely more than a scratch but it was still bleeding a little.

"Hmm," he repeated and gestured to Emily. Emily reluctantly stood up.

"Am I going to jail, Vicky?" she asked as she walked past her.

"I don't know, Emily, just tell the truth," Vicky instructed, hoping that Mitchell would find a way to keep her out of jail. Emily had lied to her, she had an affair with a guest, and she had concealed a crime, but to Vicky she was still the same sweet, shy Emily who had been such a loyal and important part of the inn for so long.

"I'll take care of her," Mitchell promised as he led Emily down the sidewalk to his own car. Vicky was walking with Aunt Ida towards the lobby when she saw Sarah walk out through the lobby door towards her.

"Vicky?" she asked with shock as she saw the bandage across her sister's neck.

"It's okay," Vicky said with a reassuring smile. "Aunt Ida cracked his head open."

"Well, it wasn't quite open," Aunt Ida said with a bit of a huff. "I have to work on my biceps. Or is it triceps? I really don't know," she shook her head with a wave of her hand.

"What happened?" Sarah asked as the flashing lights in the parking lot drew her attention. "I thought we were going to discuss this over breakfast?"

"We still will," Vicky assured her as the three women stepped inside the lobby. "But don't worry. It's all taken care of. I told you I could handle it," Vicky said with growing confidence.

"Seems like you were right," Sarah laughed and they walked into the restaurant attached to the inn. As they sat down at a table, Nicholas appeared at the entrance of the restaurant. Ida spotted him the moment he did.

"Oh, look who's here," she said with a light cluck of her tongue.

"Who's that?" Sarah asked curiously.

"That's Aunt Ida's new friend," Vicky replied with a tiny smile. "They've been sneaking around."

"We weren't sneaking," Aunt Ida huffed as she waved Nicholas over to their table. "Join us for breakfast?" she invited.

"Actually," Nicholas winced and then offered Vicky and Sarah a polite nod. "It looks like I'll be leaving tomorrow. The conference is being cancelled, and well, as long as the board approves it, I am going to be the new CEO. So, I do have a lot to get straightened out, now that the truth about Jeremy is coming out."

"You already know about that?" Vicky asked with surprise.

"You'd be surprised how fast word gets around," Nicholas chuckled. Aunt Ida tucked her cell phone deeper into her pocket and began whistling a little tune.

"Aunt Ida," Vicky sighed and shook her head but couldn't help smiling.

"If I wasn't so nosy, I wouldn't have saved your life," Aunt Ida pointed out.

"How did you know I was there?" Vicky asked curiously.

"The walls are thin," Aunt Ida reminded her.

"It's nice to meet you," Sarah finally got a word in and smiled at Nicholas. "I'm Sarah."

"Nicholas Brendan," he said as he shook her hand. "I hope that we'll be able to reschedule something similar in the next few months, if you'd be open to that."

"Absolutely," Sarah agreed with a relieved smile.

"And Ida," Nicholas turned to look at her with a charming grin. "I was hoping to steal a little of your time today."

"I would really like that," Ida replied with a quick and eager nod. "If you girls don't mind?" she glanced at Sarah and Vicky.

"Go and enjoy," Vicky insisted, and Sarah nodded in agreement.

"I'm sure that Vicky will fill me in on all the details," Sarah added.

"I will, I will," Vicky agreed. Nicholas offered Ida his arm, which she happily took. As they walked away, Vicky turned back to Sarah, prepared to tell her everything from start to finish. Before she could even open her mouth, the doors to the restaurant were thrown open, and Amanda in all her glory came strutting into the restaurant. She had a silk scarf tied around her neck to hide the bruising on it. Vicky braced herself as she knew whatever might happen next would at the very least be dramatic.

"Vicky?" she said as she walked up to the table. She was wearing a pink flowing gown that looked like it cost more than some cars.

"Yes?" Vicky asked as she looked up at her. Sarah looked up as well.

"I just wanted to let you know that what I said about suing the inn, I won't be doing that," she said quickly.

"Oh well that's good," Vicky replied in a neutral tone.

"Very good," Sarah added with more gratitude.

"After what Vicky did for me, it's the least I can do," Amanda admitted and smiled at Vicky.

"If you hadn't been there to save me, I probably wouldn't be here right now."

Vicky tried to have compassion for the woman, but it was hard, now that she knew that she and Charleston had been trying to extort money from Jeremy and all she seemed interested in was money.

"Well, Amanda, I think you should think about your safety just a little more," Vicky politely pointed out.

"And she's not the only one," Sarah added as she pointed to the bandage on Vicky's neck. "I think you are pretty good at putting yourself in harm's way."

"I didn't mean to," Vicky insisted with a sigh. "It just always seems to work that way."

"Well, it's not going to this weekend," Sarah offered a secretive smile.

"What are you talking about?" Vicky asked.

"Ladies I'm going to check out today, there are some things I need to take care of. Thank you again, Vicky," Amanda smiled at her. Vicky was sure it was the most she had seen Amanda smile since she had arrived.

"I'm sorry for your loss," Vicky murmured tenderly. She knew that on some level Amanda had to be grieving.

"Me too," Amanda admitted quietly. As she walked away from the table one of the managers was waiting for her at the door of the restaurant. He offered his arm, and she gladly took it, still teetering on those impossibly tall high heels.

"Do you think I should get a pair of those?" Vicky asked as she stared after her.

"Do you think you could walk in them?" Sarah laughed and winked at her sister.

"I could, maybe," Vicky said defensively as she folded her arms. "If I tried."

"I don't think you need high heels," Sarah said sternly. "I think you need a vacation."

"A vacation?" Vicky asked and then shrugged. "All I know for sure is that I need a nap. I'm so tired," she yawned as she said this.

"Go grab a quick one," Sarah stood up from the table. "No coffee for you this morning."

"Definitely not," Vicky agreed.

Chapter Eight

When Vicky reached the door of her apartment she paused a moment to search through her purse for her key. She usually had it out and ready but her sleepy mind was moving slower than usual. Perhaps that was why she didn't hear the footsteps approaching her from behind. She had just closed her fingers around the metal ring of her keys, when she felt a hand glide over the curve of her shoulder. She shivered at the sudden physical contact that she hadn't expected, but relaxed the moment she felt the familiar touch.

"Mitchell, you shouldn't sneak up on me," she chastised as she turned to face him. She frowned as she caught sight of what he was wearing. Mitchell was from the deep south and was a button-down shirt and trousers kind of guy. Occasionally he would wear his uniform, which Vicky did not mind at all. But it seemed that today he had gone home to change and returned in a very strange outfit. He wore a rather loud red and blue Bermuda patterned shirt, and knee-length khaki cargo shorts. As Vicky thought about it, she was fairly certain she had never seen him in shorts before.

"Well, I didn't want you to try to escape," he said calmly as he laid his hands on the curves of her hips. Vicky stared up at him, her eyes shimmering with anticipation.

"What are you up to?" she studied him inquisitively.

"That's for me to know, and for you to pack a bag," he smiled and then lowered his voice as he added. "Warm weather clothing."

"Warm weather?" Vicky asked with a chuckle. "It's fall..."

"Vicky," Mitchell pulled her a little closer, his hands still curved around her hips. "I'm taking you far, far, away from here," he murmured and kissed her softly.

"But the inn, and Sarah, and Aunt Ida..." she protested when he pulled away from the kiss.

He kissed her again, slowly and sensually. Vicky sighed and rested her shoulder against the door of her apartment. Her body began to relax and unwind as he continued the kiss. When he pulled away this time he gazed deeply into her shimmering, green eyes.

"Vicky, I'm taking you, far, far, away from here," he repeated with a mischievous smile. "Now go pack a bag."

"But I'm so tired..." she mumbled, trying to hide a yawn despite how eager she was to find out what his surprise was.

"That's fine," he nodded. "You can sleep on the way, and I'll make sure you get plenty of rest when we arrive. Do you want some help packing your bag?" he grinned, his words indicating that he was not going to be swayed.

"All right," Vicky finally gave in, though she never truly intended to fight it. She was excited, but she was still very tired. She unlocked her door and Mitchell followed her inside. He sat down on the couch in the living room as she ran back and forth collecting what she thought she might need.

"So where are we going?" she asked in the middle of her frantic gathering.

"You'll see," Mitchell replied. His words made her stop suddenly in the middle of the hallway.

"You're not going to tell me?" she asked, her eyes wide with apprehension.

"Nope," he replied and was unable to hide his spreading grin.

"Mitchell," Vicky narrowed her eyes. "The vacation is enough of a surprise, but I need to know where we're going."

"Somewhere warm," he replied and settled casually back against the couch.

"Mitchell!" Vicky growled and stalked over to him. "I need to know where we're going."

He locked eyes with her. She could tell from the gleam in his gaze that he understood why she was apprehensive, Vicky liked to know what kind of situation she was facing, but the smile on his lips indicated that he wasn't going to give in.

"I guess you'll just have to trust me," he pointed out as he held her gaze.

"I do trust you," Vicky replied with a pout. "I just want to have an idea..."

"Get packed before we miss the flight," he laughed and shook his head before looking back up at her. "Just relax, it's going to be wonderful. We need some time away together, away from all of this, where it can just be us. We need a chance to come up for air, and escape the drama. I thought you wanted this, too?" he reminded her.

"I did," Vicky replied as she sat down beside him. "I guess I just wasn't expecting it to be so sudden."

"Well, it seems to me that if we make plans, something will inevitably come up. The Sheriff is back at work and I ran things by Sarah and she said you'd be thrilled, and that you could have the time off," he added.

"Sarah helped you plan this?" Vicky asked with a mixture of amusement and amazement. Her sister usually couldn't keep anything from her.

"I needed a little advice," Mitchell explained as he trailed his fingertips along the line of her shoulder, to the curve of her elbow, before settling his hand in hers. "I wanted to make sure it would be a special experience for you. You deserve some happy memories," he added as he kissed her cheek softly. "And I want to be the one to share them with you."

Vicky melted at the tenderness in his voice and the gentleness of his touch. She stared at him for a long moment, wondering how she had ever become so lucky.

"Go pack your bag," he reminded her with a gentle squeeze of her hand. Vicky was much more energized as she finished gathering the last of her things. Within a few minutes they were in Mitchell's car on the way to the airport. Vicky questioned him a few more times about the vacation, but he remained evasive and would only wink at her. When they arrived at the airport he hurried her through security to one of the gates, without letting her see the destination on her ticket. Vicky was beside herself with curiosity. She found the fact that he was keeping it a secret very intriguing, and frustrating all at once. She hadn't been so uncertain about where she would be in the next few hours in her entire life. It was thrilling, but it was also a little intimidating.

"Where are we going?" Vicky asked again as she hung on Mitchell's arm and tried to sway his gaze towards her.

"It's a surprise, Vicky," he said with a smile as he stole a glance in her direction. "It's driving you crazy isn't it?"

Vicky drew a deep breath and tried to pretend that it wasn't. But she knew that Mitchell could see right through her. She was silent for a moment or two as they waited for the flight attendant to announce boarding. But she could only stay quiet for so long.

"Is it somewhere out of the country?" she asked with widened eyes. "No, it can't be, I don't have a passport," she murmured. Mitchell laughed quietly and tugged her closer to him so that he could wrap his arms around her waist and hold her tightly. He looked adoringly into her eyes.

"We are going to The Keys," he said wanting to be the one to tell her before they announced the destination on the plane.

"Oh, how exciting!" she exclaimed just before his lips met hers in a heavenly caress. As they kissed the announcement for boarding bellowed above them. He grabbed her hand and led her through the corridor and onto the plane. The corridor reminded her of the passageway. Vicky was accustomed to travelling in coach, she had never even considered travelling any other way, but Mitchell led her right through the first section of the plane, to first class. Vicky glanced over at him as she looked at the huge seats with plenty of leg room.

"Are you serious?" she asked with surprise.

"I told you, you could sleep on the way," he grinned as he stepped aside and let her take her seat first. Once she was settled he sat down beside her. Vicky was already enjoying the luxury of the comfortable leather seat.

"This is amazing," Vicky shook her head. "But you didn't have to do all of this, just for me," she frowned as she looked over at him.

"Correction," Mitchell replied with absolute confidence. "I don't have to do just this," he smiled at her and stole a light kiss from her lips. "Vicky, there's nothing in the world that I would love more than being able to give you a gift that expresses just how I feel about you. Unfortunately, there's not much that can express it, so hopefully this will do."

Vicky settled back thoughtfully in her seat and studied Mitchell. She'd never met a man who she was so comfortable with and who was intent on expressing his feelings. It amazed her that he could simply know that he adored her. He never seemed to question it. Vicky adored him in return, but there was always a nervous part of her, wondering if he would grow tired of her, or if she would step out of bounds a little too far with her amateur sleuthing. He never gave her a reason to doubt him, and she was starting to realize maybe she would never need to.

Mitchell rubbed her hand in a slow circular pattern as her eyes slipped shut. He eased her into an incredibly peaceful slumber. When Vicky opened her eyes again, the plane was making its descent. She was a little disappointed that she had slept through the entire flight, but she felt so much better. As she looked out the window all she could see was clear aqua tinted water. Her eyes widened at the sight of it and she took a sharp breath at the beauty.

"Almost there," Mitchell said and gave her hand a light pat.

***

"Oh this is great," Vicky said with a wide grin after they had battled their way off the plane and through the busy airport.

"I know it's not Paris, but..."

"It's perfect," Vicky hugged him tightly around the waist and had to stop herself from jumping up and down like a little girl. "Oh, we can go swimming!" she said gleefully. "We can lay on the beach! We can..."

"Do anything you want," he replied as he led her out of the airport to the car that was waiting for them. "But first, there's one thing I want to do," he said quietly. It was nearing sunset when he parked at one of the many white, sandy beaches. He took her hand and they walked through the sand. Vicky eagerly abandoned her shoes and sunk her feet into the surprisingly soft sand.

"This is amazing," Vicky said as she looked out over the calm water that stretched as far as she could see.

"This beauty," Mitchell said quietly as he stretched his arm out across the view in front of them, where the sun had slowly begun to set, "is the closest thing that compares to the way I feel, when I'm with you," he murmured and slid his arm around her waist. "I spent some time here as a kid, and from the first day I met you, you reminded me of these sunsets, of the endless calm water, of the beauty that can't be recreated, not with a paintbrush, not with a camera, not with anything but the real thing," he tilted his head slightly to look down into her eyes.

"Mitchell, how did I ever get so lucky to find someone as wonderful as you?" Vicky asked.

"I waited a long time for you to find me," he reminded her and the kiss they shared coincided with the exact moment of the sunset setting the horizon ablaze with its multitude of colors.

The End

More Cozy Mysteries by Cindy Bell

Heavenly Highland Inn Cozy Mystery Series

Murdering the Roses

Dead in the Daisies

Bekki the Beautician Cozy Mystery Series

Hairspray and Homicide

A Dyed Blonde and a Dead Body

Mascara and Murder

Pageant and Poison

Conditioner and a Corpse

Makeup, Mistletoe and Murder

21150934R00084

Printed in Great Britain
by Amazon